Bound by a Secret

Jolene Navarro

LOVE INSPIRED

INSPIRATIONAL ROMANCE

LOVE INSPIRED®

INSPIRATIONAL ROMANCE

Recycling programs
for this product may
not exist in your area.

ISBN-13: 978-1-335-58629-2

Bound by a Secret

Love Inspired
22 Adelaide St. West, 41st Floor
Toronto, Ontario M5H 4E3, Canada
www.LoveInspired.com

Printed in U.S.A.

Be not deceived; God is not mocked:
for whatsoever a man soweth, that shall he also
reap. For he that soweth to his flesh shall of the
flesh reap corruption; but he that soweth to the
Spirit shall of the Spirit reap life everlasting.
And let us not be weary in well doing:
for in due season we shall reap, if we faint not.
—*Galatians* 6:7–9

This book is dedicated to all the
four-legged family members who have given us
unconditional love throughout the years.
Sam took me from kinder to my senior year.
Jazz, my cocker spaniel, loved me through
all my college years and into marriage
and motherhood. Our rescue dog, Besty,
helped raise my kids. There have been more,
and they all have a special place in my heart.
Finn and Bliss were borrowed from Teri Wilson.

Chapter One

Greyson McKinsey rolled his neck and stared at the Texas sky above him. The perfect cerulean blue stretched on forever, with only a few spots of white to break it up. A swirl of dust danced across the road leading to his new house. It was late January, but it felt more like July.

January was a hard month to get through. Soon the calendar would reach the anniversary of the day he'd met Jessica. Nothing he did would stop it. Being sentimental, she'd wanted to get married on the anniversary of the day they'd met. And they had. They would have been celebrating eleven years together, but now the date marked the day she was murdered.

Being busy was good. Anything to avoid the fact that he had failed her.

In town this morning, the talk was all about the weather. Weather was always a safe topic. He heard that it was drier than the heart of a haystack. Not to be outdone, another cowboy complained about it being windier than a fifty-pound bag of whistling lips. A dry snort escaped past his frustration. That one didn't even make sense.

He enjoyed the bygone Texas sayings he heard from the ancient cowboys playing dominoes at the local feed store. It was a different lifestyle from the ones he had lived in San Francisco or Charlotte. Shaking his head, he lowered his gaze and studied the wide horizon that was the new home the US Marshals Service helped him find since the end of his wife's murder trial.

The man who had murdered his wife was behind bars. All Jessica had been guilty of was protecting his children from his violence. But that man believed she had done him wrong, and vengeance was his way of life. Ultimately his wife had won in the courts and his children were removed from the man's home, but she had paid the highest price. To protect his girls, they were moved into the witness protection program until it was safe. The US Marshal, Diego, had told him it could be anywhere from a few years to decades. Possibly the rest of their lives.

He'd never thought he'd live in Texas, especially in such a rural area. But the small coastal town where families had stories that spanned generations had started to feel like home. He wanted to belong here, but after losing his wife and going into hiding, he didn't know if he'd ever truly feel at peace again. They'd had to move twice so far, and he was tired. Would they be able to stay here, or would he have to uproot the girls again?

Turning to his twins, he frowned. They didn't understand why they had a new last name, why they had to move again. They weren't adjusting to their new environment as easily as he was. The first four years of their life had been perfect. Now, for their protection, he had to give them false memories mixed in with bits of truth. He refused to completely wipe their mother from their history. It was a tough balancing act.

For the last three years they had lived in Charlotte while he traveled back and forth to testify. But they didn't know that. All they knew was they had lost their mother to an accident, their dad had to go to work a lot, and now they had lost their friends.

Currently, the twins sat on the porch swing

under the window. Heads down, their legs swung in identical rhythm. The pair of Cavalier King Charles Spaniel pups he had given them last month as birthday gifts looked just as dejected under the bench.

Purple stains covered the girls' small hands and were smeared around the black noses of the pups. The same purple that was also streaked across the new boards he had just replaced on the front porch. After working on the water pump, he hadn't applied the PVC primer right away. At least the stuff wasn't toxic.

He sighed. The twins had wanted his attention, and now they had it.

The need to yell, rant and throw something, boiled underneath the surface. But he knew it wasn't the girls that caused this anger. He glanced at his watch. Nothing was going as planned this morning.

The water pump had busted. The new nanny was now twenty minutes late. And he had another appointment scheduled in ten minutes. Jessica had kept everything running smoothly. He didn't know how she had done it, along with working as a child advocate. Now he was doing it all alone and failing. The general unfairness of life had him on edge.

The girls wanted to talk to their friends at their last school, and they didn't understand why it wasn't allowed. They wanted their mom, but instead they were stuck with their workaholic father, who wasn't the same man he'd been with his wife. He wanted to be better for them, but his old confidence had vanished when he'd lost Jessica. He was a stranger in his own skin.

With a deep breath and a small prayer, he kneeled before the most precious gifts in his life. Laying a gentle hand on each of the girls' legs, he studied their small faces. Nope, not all his frustration had to do with the extra work his daughters had just created. "Are you allowed to get into my supplies without asking?"

"No, Daddy." They answered in unison in the same voice.

"But, Daddy." Evelyn, the older twin, looked up at him, her eyes so much like her mother's that his heart twisted. There wasn't a day that he didn't miss her. "We wanted to help and make it pretty."

Even though they had only been four, his daughters had to feel that loss of their mother twice as much. Jessica had been the primary parent while he had been busy building his company.

Now all they had was him, and he only had them to keep him going. "I want you to help, but you need to talk to me first. That was not paint you used. It's a primer for PVC pipes, and it won't come off." He gave his head a sad shake, but he couldn't resist teasing them. "Your hands might be purple forever."

Eyes wide, they looked at him, then to their hands. Flipping his wrist, he noted that the nanny was now twenty-five minutes late. He had really been optimistic that having help with the girls would reduce the stress for them all. The Marshals had vetted her. Being late or just not showing for a scheduled time had always been a pet peeve with him. It was rude and disrespectful of other people's time.

He sighed. "Girls, don't worry. We'll get it off. I have an appointment at the barn. You'll have to go with me, but you're in time-out. No talking. No playing. Finn and Bliss will be in their crate."

"Daddy, they'll be good. Please let them come. We promise to sit very still. They will too."

His heart broke. They were so sweet. He was messing this whole parenting thing up. Glancing over at the purple marks, he pulled his lips to the side. What would Jessica do with the girls?

"You're going to have to wash the porch, but I'll have to strip the wood to remove the marks. We'll have to figure out other things for you to do."

Before he could say any more, he heard tires on their graveled road. He straightened and turned. Was it the no-show nanny or the carpenter?

Going to the edge of the porch, he waited for the small, neat Ford Focus to come down the drive. A woman was driving, and she parked right in front of the house. Finally, the nanny. He might just make his appointment with the carpenter.

The woman who got out wasn't quite what he was expecting. She was younger, for a start. But she had a vibe of being no-nonsense and ready to take control. Her sturdy overalls were a washed-out pink, and her dark hair was pulled tight in two long braids.

She definitely looked as if she was ready to do anything to get the job done. Hopefully, she would be the supernanny he'd been praying for.

With a smile at the girls, she came forward and held her hand out to him. "Hello, Mr. McKinsey. Sorry I'm late. The road was blocked due to an accident."

"I'm happy you're finally here. I've heard

great things about you. Nothing but good reports." Most importantly, the background checks the US Marshals completed were super clean. He glanced over his shoulder at the twins. "As you can see, we could really use your expertise. I'm late for another appointment, so if you'd follow me? Girls, come on. This is Evelyn and Abilene. They're great kids. But you have to keep a close eye on them. They're very inquisitive. They like to help and get highly creative."

He paused as he stepped over the purple marks. "I took my eyes off of them for less than five minutes while I was texting, and this happened."

Her eyebrows went up. "Purple primer? I've never seen it used this way before. That's interesting." She smiled at the girls. "Can you tell me about your painting?"

Both girls perked up. Even the puppies they held wagged their tails, as if excited someone had asked. "These are our friends and teachers at our old school," Evelyn said.

Abilene moved to the other end. "The one alone without a face is our mom. Purple was her favorite color. And she loved wildflowers. We painted them here by the front door so every time we come in and out of the house, we'll remember them." Head lowered, her big eyes peeked out from under her bangs.

He stopped and looked back at the purple people and flowers dancing across his new boards. He hadn't even bothered to ask the girls what the paintings meant to them.

What did he do now? That was the most heartbreaking thing they could have said. He felt even worse.

The new nanny nodded. "Remembering the people we love is important, but you have to get approval when you do art, otherwise it's vandalism."

"Vandalism?" they asked in stereo.

"Yup. If you put up a mural where people want it, then it's art, but if you mark up a building where people don't want it, it's vandalism. That's against the law."

The girls stared at each other, then back to this amazing nanny. No wonder her recommendations all raved about her.

She had her hands in her pockets. "I imagine that if you talked to your dad about what you want to do, he would find the perfect place for your mural. You could help someone create a mural remembering all the people that you want to remember. Maybe not here at the front door, but perhaps in your room or somewhere in one of the barns?"

The girls lit up at this thought and turned to him.

Eyebrows high, she looked at him and made a face that said she was sorry and hoped she hadn't overstepped. Clearing her throat, she touched Evelyn's shoulder. "But that's totally up to your dad. He knows what needs to happen on the farm."

He sighed. Yup, she was a regular Mary Poppins, and that was what they needed right now. Someone who would take the time to understand the complicated situation. And for the first time in several years, he felt hopeful. "You wouldn't know the best way to remove purple stains from kids and dogs, would you?"

"Do you have baking soda and cooking oil?"

Of course she had a recipe to solve the problem. "I do. Follow me." He opened the door and waited for them to come inside. "She's right, girls. We'll figure something out." And not make it public.

They hugged him, and for a minute he was engulfed in girls and puppies. "Thank you, Daddy."

"But that doesn't mean you're not in trouble for getting the primer and putting it somewhere it wasn't supposed to be," he reminded them. They stepped back and nodded.

"Okay. Come on." He couldn't let the emotions swallow him up right now. If he could get the twins settled with the new nanny, he could still make his next appointment.

Walking through the living room, he made a mental note to unpack the new boxes stacked against the wall. All new stuff had been ordered, and he didn't even know what it was. He didn't slow down as he passed through the dining room, where more bins needed sorting. On the other side of the huge family kitchen was a large utility room.

It didn't take them as long as he thought it would to remove the stains. He sent a text to Reno, the carpenter, that he would be late.

Once the purple was dealt with, he went to the large sliding barn doors on the other side of the kitchen and pushed them open.

One of the reasons he'd wanted this property was the open floor plan. Downstairs was a large family room that now served as a playroom. It could be seen from the kitchen or living room when the sliding doors were pushed back or closed off when they didn't need it.

Right now, the room was a disaster. "Because of the extra work you created outside, you have to make sure this room is organized and everything is in its place." He pointed to the wall of shelves and all the scattered storage units.

Currently, most of the containers were stacked on top of each other to create a wall around a group of dolls and stuffed animals. It was so cluttered that there was no floor visible, not even a path to get through the room. When had he lost control? A weary sigh slipped out. Had he ever been in control?

"You were supposed to be here cleaning. Now you are going to stay in here until everything is in its proper place. No stuffing or hiding allowed. You will get a lunch break, and I expect it to be done by dinner." He looked at the person who was, he'd been assured, the best nanny available. "You can guide them and make suggestions, but they have to do all the work."

She stared at him with total shock on her face, and after a few blinks she scanned the room. "This is what you wanted me to do? Reno had said you wanted the old barns restored."

"The barns?" *Oh no.* He had a horrible realization. "You're not Sarah Clemens?"

She wrinkled her nose. "No, I'm... Savannah Espinoza."

With a smile, he had to ask, "You're not sure?"

With another glance at the disaster area, she shook her head. "You seem to need Sarah much more than you need me."

One hand went to his hair before he could stop it. He had been trying to break that habit. "Sorry. It's been a long day. Already. There was a nanny that never showed. I was expecting her at nine." He looked at his watch. "Reno and his partner were scheduled for nine forty-five at the barns. When you drove up alone, I was so grateful that the nanny had shown I didn't even give you a proper greeting."

She nodded. "I saw you on the porch, so I figured I would pull up here instead of driving out to the barns. I take it Reno didn't tell you his partner was his sister. He thinks it's fun to surprise people with me. He's also a volunteer fireman and was called to the accident that had the road blocked. So I came on ahead. He'll join us as soon as the road—" Her eyes went wide. "Oh no. Do you think that was Sarah, your nanny?" She pulled out her phone. "I can call my brothers. They were both there. Reno and Bridges. He's a deputy." She sent out a text.

He ran his fingers through his hair again. "That would explain why she didn't return my text or calls. Now I feel horrible for being so agitated at her."

He lifted up a small prayer for her safety. "You drove past. Did everything look okay? Did you see her?"

"I couldn't see anything around the fire truck. There was an ambulance." Her phone pinged, and she looked at it. "They had to cut her out of the car, but she was talking. She's on the way to the hospital. Reno said she was banged up, but it's nothing life-threatening."

He closed his eyes. They were all silent for a minute. "Okay. I'll follow up with her later. For now, it looks like we're all going to the barn."

The girls' faces lit up. He gave them a stern glare. They quickly lowered their chins and pulled the pups closer. "You're still in trouble, and there will be no playing or talking."

"Yes, Daddy."

They followed him through the house and out the front door. He stopped at the edge of the porch. "Do you want to go with me? It doesn't look as if you have any tools with you." He eyed her small car. Another reason it hadn't occurred to him that she wasn't the nanny.

"So did you think I was the nanny because I'm a woman or because I'm driving my sister's car?" She was grinning at him like it was a joke.

"No," was his instinctive reply.

"Daddy says girls can be whatever they want, but for some jobs they have to work harder because people won't give them a fair chance," Evelyn offered.

The corner of his mouth pulled. "The little car did give me nanny vibes. It doesn't have the look of a carpenter's car. Don't you have to drive a van or truck to store your supplies?"

She laughed. "Fair enough. My truck busted a belt, and I hate being late, so I borrowed my sister's car. She's a midwife. I'll go with you."

Smiling, he held the front passenger door open. "You'll be the first person to get a guided tour of Seeds of Faith Farm."

Shutting the door, he helped the girls in and went to the driver's side, singing under his breath. When he got in, his daughters started singing with him. At the end of the song, they clapped.

"Daddy, we miss singing with you," Abilene said softly.

Bouncing, Evelyn asked, "Can we do it again?"

He blinked. They were right. When was the last time he'd sung? He glanced at his passenger. She smiled back. "Please don't stop on my account. I love singing. I'm not any good, but I say the louder, the better."

The girls started up, and she joined them. But he couldn't. He made sure to smile so as not to dampen their joy, but he hadn't sung since Jessica was murdered.

Why would he start today?

Chapter Two

Savannah made herself look out the window. She had never seen anyone go from joy to sobriety so fast. She wanted to reach out and comfort him. Gossips were arguing about his place of origin. They had him from all over the country. Rumors in town were all about the good-looking single dad who had somehow managed to buy the Boone farm, and no one could figure out how. He was presenting a real challenge. People either wanted him to go back to where he came from, or they had the perfect match for him.

They also speculated about his missing wife. Some said he lost her to cancer, others heard it was an accident. The most popular rumor said she had left him and the girls when he bought the farm here in Texas.

There hadn't been a word about a rich singing voice or the deep sadness in his eyes. It must have been the singing. She couldn't physically reach out, but she could distract him.

"Everyone in town is trying to figure out how you convinced the Boone family to sell. Grandpa Boone bragged he'd never sell to developers or to anyone from California. So you say you're from California?"

He frowned. "I never said that. No." The muscle that ran along his angled jawbone flexed. He navigated the SUV over a rough dirt road, and they bumped along to the biggest barn on the other side of the first field. He glanced at her, then looked back at the road. It didn't seem as if he wanted to share.

Evelyn leaned as far as her seat belt allowed. "Daddy said we had family here in Texas and he wanted to come back."

That surprised her. "You did? *McKinsey*?" She ran the name through all the files she could access in her brain. "That name doesn't sound familiar. In a small town, we keep family names around for generations." She'd have to ask her mother. She'd know.

"Not this part of Texas." Instead of relaxing his mood, he cut a glare to the rearview. His knuckles went white around the steering wheel. "It was a distant cousin's farm. I'm a very private person and would rather not talk about it." His face was tight and completely closed off.

Why would that upset him? "Okay." She frowned. That was weird, right? Or was she just overly sensitive since the Colin, or James as she later found out, debacle. Once a boyfriend lies about his name, it's easy to see lies everywhere. Even when it turned out he was undercover, it had still hurt. "I'm surprised that's not part of the town gossip. And don't worry, I won't be adding to it. I never talk to anyone, anyway. I totally agree about people minding their own business."

"Thank you. I appreciate it." He glanced at the girls again.

"Sorry, Daddy. I forgot I'm not supposed to talk about our family."

He grimaced, then glanced at Savannah. "It's okay. My goal is to lie low and raise my girls as we grow some wildflowers. No drama. No gossip."

"I won't say anything, but I must warn you, it's a very small town. Less than five hundred people. You're going to be talked about. Anything new is going to travel faster than a hawk going after a single chick. If they don't have all the information, they'll make it up. Trust me, and don't ask how I know." It was humiliating, and she hated seeing the pity in everyone's eyes. He probably had some sad, tragic story and felt the same way.

"I'm sure anything they create will be more interesting than the truth." He parked at a large, three-story barn. It had a classic steeple with a hayloft and then a long slant on the right twice as long as the one on the left. It was a beautiful structure—and it needed lots of attention.

Cutting the engine, he turned to her. "What would I hear about you in town if I was interested in gossip?"

"Oh, if you hang out long enough, you'll hear all about the odd Espinoza girl. Let's see. One, I wasted time and money getting a useless master's degree in sculpture." She counted off on her fingers. "Two, I'm not the smartest of my siblings. I gave all my money away to someone I shouldn't have trusted. Three, I'm nothing like the community pillars my siblings are. If there are any good works being done in town or if anyone's helping others, my mother and sisters are in the middle of it. One brother is a deputy, and the other is working on becoming a firefighter and will literally stop everything to save a kitten in a tree. They can't figure out what went wrong with me. I missed the nurturing, do-good-works gene."

Clasping her hands together, she gave him a big smile. "But they do admit that I'm very talented with wood, just like my father. It's my one and only useful gift." She got out of his SUV and surveyed the grand old barn. Once again, she'd opened her mouth and said too much.

He walked around and stood next to her. They took in the details of the century-old barn. "The last bit is a good thing for you, Mr. McKinsey. That is a great deal of wood that needs help."

He nodded. "Your brother did tell me his partner was a master carpenter. I wasn't expecting a master's degree. Let me get the girls, and we'll walk through it. This is the barn I want to focus on. It will be the face of the farm. I hope to use it to impress my commercial clients to show off the current crops and the possibilities with native landscaping on a large scale."

He shepherded his girls and their pups through the wide double doors, and she followed. Immediately her eyes went up. In the center of the space, the ceiling peaked in a network of heavy support beams. Streaks of sun highlighted the dust dancing high above them. The back of the barn had a large, open loft where the railing had given way. A bird abandoned its nest and flew out the hay door. The old-time craftsmanship took her breath.

"It's beautiful, isn't it? Will we be able to save most of it, or is it too far gone? Tell me this beauty can be saved."

"Oh, I can rescue your lady, and she should be completely restored. The question is, can you afford it? This would also make a great event location. Reno said your first harvest is end of May?" She walked to the ladder that went to the loft and tested it. "Nope. Make sure the girls don't climb anything. Some of the wood might not be as sturdy as it looks."

Touching the main beam, she looked up into the loft. "Unfortunately, there are times it's more cost-effective to bulldoze and start from scratch."

"Event venues are not my thing. I'd like to be as private as possible. Dealing with buyers and distributors is a far cry from a free-for-all. I'm not sure I want to do something so open to the public. I thought—" His phone chimed, and he looked at the caller ID. "It's the agency that Sarah works with." He stepped away to take the call.

She ran her hand along the old wood, imagining all the people who had worked here and their stories.

He came back with a grim expression.

"Sarah's okay, but she was banged up pretty bad. It'll be six to eight weeks before she can report back to work. They're going to send me someone else." Hands crammed into his pockets, he looked at his daughters, who were still standing quietly beside them. "I don't like having people I know nothing about around the girls."

"That's tough. But she's coming from the agency, so there are background checks and references, right?"

"Yeah, but not from people I know." He shook his head. The Marshals had vetted Sarah. He had wanted to make sure the nanny had no ties to the man who had killed Jessica after she had testified on behalf of his children.

That monster had lost all rights to them, and then in the courtroom he had threatened Jessica. Then he had followed through and shot Jessica in the middle of the day in front of an art gallery. He'd need to call Diego, the Marshal in charge of his case, as soon as he got back to the house.

He sighed. For now, his focus was on the barn and this woman who intrigued him. "So did you get any good news from the walls you were talking to?"

She blushed. "You saw that? I have a habit

of talking to the wood I'm working with. It has a life and a history older than us. We might have to replace some of the planks, but we could salvage most of it and incorporate it into other projects. The biggest problem might be getting lumber delivered in time. Orders are running behind." Moving around the ladder, she opened the sliding door to the rock partition of the barn. The large area was damp and moldy. Old barrels and forgotten sacks filled the long-disused stalls. She pulled out her small notebook and started writing.

"Girls, sit on that bench and don't move. Do you understand?"

"Yes, Daddy."

She turned. Evelyn and Abilene still clung to their wiggly puppies, but they sat on the bench. Greyson followed her. "My goal is to save as much as we can. I was hoping we could just do some remodeling without destroying the bones. What do you think?"

"My heart tells me to do everything to restore it to its glorious past. But until we know what we have, there's no telling." She dug at the base of a support pole with her fingertips and looked up to the ceiling.

"I want to save as much of the original materials as possible within my budget. I don't have a clue what to ask or look for."

She nodded. "What about repurposing wood we need to remove for structural reasons? It would keep the history of the property alive and save money."

"I like the way you think. Come on. Let me show you what I believe is the old granary and foaling area."

As they walked through the rest of the space, he shared his hopes and vision for the business. He saw this as the showplace to bring wholesalers and stack the packaged seeds that were ready for sale.

Savannah asked questions and took notes. Once they'd finished exploring every dark and forgotten corner, they retrieved the girls and went to the next two barns. They were newer and much more commercial-looking. These would be the harvesting, sorting and packaging barns.

"In the front of the farm, I have two fields already planted for this spring. I just need rain. All-new cedar fencing is going around the back of the fields along the dirt roads. Once the fields start blooming, I know they'll gain attention, so it's important to keep people off of them." Driving along the outer fence line, he took them back to the front of the property.

"You know, this could easily be a destination. People will drive a distance to see a giant field of wildflowers." She could see families taking pictures and enjoying the day together.

"I just want to focus on my commercial buyers. In the front fields, we'll run some horses and a small herd of grazing long-horns." He stopped the SUV and scanned the horizon.

The light in his eyes was enough for her to see his vision. "Very Texan." She smiled. "What made you want to come back to Texas to build a wildflower-seed farm? I've never heard of that type of crop."

"Exactly. I was, um…" he pulled his lips tight as if trying to find the words "…trying to figure out what to do next in my life. And a discussion about wildflowers with a past client gave me an idea. There's something majestic about flowers unaltered by man. We're naturally drawn to the gifts God has given us. And they're hard to find as a large-scale crop."

The girls leaned forward. "They were Mommy's favorite flowers. We would stop whenever she saw some. And Daddy would bring them home to her too," Abilene cheerily added.

His fingers tightened around the steering wheel.

Evelyn hit her sister, then followed it with a glare. Savannah looked forward. It wasn't her place to say anything, but the girls didn't seem to be able to talk about their mom without upsetting Greyson. The story had to be a tragic one to evoke that kind of reaction. Or he was hiding something. Her gut told her he wasn't a liar, but she wasn't a good judge. Either way it couldn't be mentally healthy for the girls or for him. Not her business, though.

"So Reno said you already have partners for retailing the seeds. But you also want a storefront here that will open this spring?"

He relaxed and put the car in Drive. "Yes. Not for the public but for commercial clients. The space will show varieties and options for large landscape projects. I wanted to start small, but by next fall I should have all twenty acres planted so we can have a bigger harvest next spring. I'd like to include native grasses that are good for wildlife and domestic stock. The seeds need to be in the ground in September and then pray for October and November rain. In Cal—in the past, I've worked with commercial architects and landscapers. Their clients are requesting wildflowers, but they're just about impossible to find on a large commercial scale. There's a family in the Hill Country, Alvarado Farms, who's growing them on a small scale, and I'll be working with them to develop a bigger market."

They were all silent as they drove back to the house. "That was more than you asked for." When they stopped, he turned to her. "You asked me questions, so I have one for you. If you have a master's degree in sculpture, what do you make? Do you have a gallery?"

"I love working with natural elements. My favorite is driftwood. I've made some decorative abstract pieces I love, but I kept going back to functional pieces that have an organic flair. Is it a table or an art piece? That kind of thing. But that's on hold for now."

He raised an eyebrow, and she sighed. Most people didn't get it. Even in her art program, they'd questioned her passion. It wasn't going to set the art world on fire. But she could spend hours sanding wood to find hidden forms and shapes, and putting an original piece together to create something new gave her a thrill each time. It was a wonderful escape, but as her family liked to remind her, she had to live in the real world. Had to pay bills and plan for retirement.

"Then, the carpentry makes sense. Where do you sell your work?"

She twisted her mouth to the side. Another disappointment and failure on her part. "I don't. The work requires a large space with expensive tools. Right now, I have sketch-books full of ideas ready to execute. Some-day, that's the plan." She also needed to reignite her creative spark. It was gone.

He paused as he opened the door. "I get it, but you know, *Someday* isn't an actual day of the week." He winked. "*Someday* is always lost in the future. You'd have a better chance if you picked a day that exists in writing. I know it's overwhelming, but— Sorry. I have no business giving advice." He snorted and looked away. "I kept saying *Someday*." He turned to her, his sadness so deep it hit her like a physical punch. "While I was busy, some-day slipped past, and I'll never get it back."

Stepping out of the SUV, he moved to the back and helped his girls down. "Let's go inside. My little rabble rousers here owe me time, and there's a playroom to organize." With the twins holding his hands and the spaniels trotting beside them, he went up the steps. "Is it okay if we discuss the plans I have for the farm and my budget while they're tak-ing care of their business?"

"Sure."

The girls smiled at her, then went inside the farmhouse with their father. There was more to his story than just a single dad starting a new business, but it wasn't her place to dig. She was here to fix his barns. She and Reno had a job to do, and it had nothing to do with getting to know Greyson and his little girls.

She gave the long driveway a glance. Where was her brother? She didn't need any more bonding time with this family.

Somehow, she had already managed to get involved with helping the girls. Despite everyone in her family knowing she wasn't good with kids. Usually, she was awkward and uncomfortable around them, but the twins seemed so lost.

Her phone vibrated. A text said Reno was on his way.

That was good. He was the people person. Everyone in her family was better at social interaction than she was. She had somehow missed the outgoing gene the rest of her family had inherited tenfold. He would also do a great job helping the twins clean the porch: he was still basically a big kid himself.

Going into the house, she followed the sound of Greyson's voice, but then she slowed down. Walking alone through the hallway, she took the opportunity to really take in his home. There were no pictures, and each room contained several boxes still waiting to be unpacked.

There was basic furniture, but nothing else. Unopened crates served as end tables. It was a stark contrast to the home she grew up in and had just moved back into.

In her mom's home, curtains her sisters had made hung over the windows, artwork by the kids and grandkids decorated the walls, and cozy homemade afghans and quilts invited you to curl up in the family room and visit.

There were also pictures. Lots of pictures. Some she considered embarrassing proof of her awkward stages, but they were there to remind everyone of the love and joy family brought. Maybe Greyson had just been too busy to settle in, but her gut told her it was more than that.

There was a deep-rooted reason he kept to himself, but it wasn't her place to learn what that was. She was here for a job: to restore his old barns, not to redecorate his home. Her mother or sisters were the ones who took over people's lives and fixed them.

Anyway, Greyson was an adult and could take care of himself. She walked past the large farm table, noting the neatly stacked boxes that left nowhere to sit for a family meal.

That was okay. Not all families sat at a table. When she was living with her art community, they'd never used the table to eat. It was always covered with creative projects in progress. Instead, they would gather in the living areas, sitting on the rugs or sofa. It wasn't how her family had done mealtimes, but it was fun, and she had enjoyed it. Greyson seemed to be a good father, and he didn't need her to tell him what to do with his family.

But the house was so sterile. The dining room and kitchen were freshly painted a light gray, with no added color or joy. Then she stepped through the threshold of the double doors and down into the girls' playroom. This was the color of chaos. She grinned. How could these two spaces exist in the same house?

Greyson stood in the middle with his hands on his hips and scanned the area. "First, put Bliss and Finn in their crate."

"Daddy!"

"Abilene." Even she stood straighter at his tone. The girls stepped over toys and around objects to the far side of the room. Covered by pink and purple blankets was a table that had a large crate built in underneath. It was the prettiest dog crate she had ever seen. Bliss and Finn whined, and the girls looked as if they were about to cry.

Greyson dropped his head and was silent for a minute. Her guess would be that he was praying for patience. Raising his chin, he took a deep breath and went to the girls. "They're right here. We'll give them a treat. If they're out, then you'll get distracted from your job. And they're still chewing on everything. Another reason to keep your room clean. They have no way of knowing what their toys are in all this mess. It's your responsibility to teach them." He picked up a shoe with the back chewed off. "If this shoe was where it belonged, they would not have eaten the back off it."

Hands clasped in front of them, the girls nodded. "Daddy, we don't know where to start," Evelyn said as both girls looked at the swamp of toys, clothes and games.

He looked just as overwhelmed as he scanned the room.

Savannah stepped down and kneeled by the puppies. "Give these guys a treat for being good pups in their crate and make sure they have something to chew on," she told them. "Then unstack the cubbies from the fort you made."

The girls went to the shelf and got a jar of treats. It was next to what she assumed was their jar of fun money. With the dogs taken care of, the girls and their father looked to her, waiting for instruction. Well, she couldn't be one of seven kids without learning some skills in managing kids and cleanup time.

"First, find one type of item, like Legos." She picked up a yellow one and handed it to Abilene. "And gather them all up in one cubby. What could be next?"

Evelyn picked a blue container from their wall. "I can find all the doll clothes."

Abilene lowered a pink cubby from the tower. "After the Legos, I'll find all our dinosaurs. It's a treasure hunt." The girls dug through the piles of toys and clothes, competing to see who could fill their box first.

Greyson gave her a lopsided grin and shook his head. "Thank you. I had no idea where to start. Are you sure you don't want the nanny job?"

The laugh came out in a gawky burst, and her neck grew warm. Why was she so awkward? "I'm one of seven, so I had to pick up some helpful tricks along the way, but if you're looking for domestic help—" she shook her head "—you have the wrong Espinoza. Do they have music? When I clean, I listen to music."

"Good idea." He went over to the white, floor-to-ceiling shelves, and a happy sing-along song came from the walls. The girls smiled and hurried around the room, trying to outdo each other. Moving to the door, he gestured for her to go through to the kitchen.

"Want something to drink?" He opened the refrigerator door. Finally, some artwork. She smiled at a drawing of puppies playing under trees. Another had a person whom she assumed was their dad with a hat, standing in the middle of flowers. *Seeds of Faith* was written across the top.

"There's lemonade, Dr. Pepper and water." He grabbed a glass bottle of soda.

"I'll take one of those." She pulled out her laptop. "Reno should be here any minute, and we can get into the details of the project."

He twisted the top off and handed her the drink, then got another for himself. Sitting down at the edge of the large woodblock island, he opened his laptop. "Sounds good. Let me pull up the floor plans and ideas I have for the old barn. I'm hoping to eventually add tables and custom shelving. I want to plan for those now, so they'll be easier to add later."

He concentrated on the computer, and the muscles in his forearm flexed as he worked over the keys. His long-sleeved T-shirt was pushed up to his elbows, and his thick hair was mussed from his fingers running through it earlier. He slid on a pair of black-rimmed glasses and leaned closer to the screen.

Her heart gave a flutter at the picture he made. The glasses pushed her right over the edge.

There was a knock on the door, and she jumped up. "That should be Reno. I'll go let him in."

Out of breath and flushed, she rushed to open the door, then stepped back to let the little brother who stood five inches taller than her into the house. "Hello, Reno. Come in. Come in."

"Hey, sis." He frowned. "Are you okay?"

Trying to get whatever had hit her under control, she shrugged. "I'm great. Why are you asking?"

He raised one brow. "You looked rattled, and you're acting like the lady of the house." Stepping past her, he searched the area for Greyson.

"Where are you hiding Mr. McKinsey?"

She rolled her eyes. "Greyson's in the kitchen. He was pulling information up on his laptop, so I went for the door."

"Greyson?" He grinned as he walked past her. "Maybe you don't need me after all."

"Don't be stupid. He's very nice and not much older than us, so he asked me to call him by his first name." She bit her lip to stop herself talking. Being defensive would call attention to her unexpected reaction to Greyson in glasses. *But he's so cute*, the internal girlie voice she hadn't heard from in a long time whined. *Stop it*.

"Savannah, are you sure you're okay?"

With a smile, as though nothing was weird, she nodded. "This way."

He followed her down the hall. "I thought they'd been here for a couple of months now." He was looking at all the walls of unpacked boxes.

"Yes." Feeling uncomfortably protective over a man she just met, Savannah glared at her little brother. "He's been very busy."

Greyson stood when they entered the kitchen area, and the men shook hands. As they sat around the island, Savannah let Reno do the talking while she took notes to go over with him later. It took all her energy to focus on what was being said.

When they'd finished working out the details, Greyson invited them to stay for lunch.

"No. We have another appointment," she blurted out before Reno could accept. The more time she spent with Greyson McKinsey and his daughters, the more likely it was that these weird feelings would become weirder, and no one needed that.

Her brother gave her a confused glance but

then smiled at Greyson. "Sorry, man. Next time."

With a quick goodbye to the girls, she fled the house as fast as she could. She wasn't in the mood to explain her behavior to her brother. She wouldn't be able to, anyway. There was no explanation for her reaction.

This was a big job for their new business, and she couldn't mess it up.

"What was that all about?" Reno was right behind her. She gritted her teeth, then pulled the car door open.

"What? Whatever you want to talk about, can we do it later? I do have an appointment, and I need to go."

His gaze narrowed in on her. "Something is wrong with you. Do you need my help? Is it Colin? Or James? Whatever his name was. Is he bothering you? Or any of those art people?"

Oh, her sweet baby brother.

The part only Reno knew because she had been too embarrassed by her foolishness to tell the rest of her family was about Colin who she'd found out later was actually James. The man she thought she was in love with was just an undercover cop playing a role, and she had been naive enough not to see the signs. He had lied to her about everything, even his real name. As far as the rest of the family knew, it was just a bad breakup and she was ready to grow up and get a real job.

"No. They've all forgotten about me. I just feel a little out of sorts. I do have somewhere to be." Not an appointment, but she needed time alone. "I'll see you at home." They now shared the garage apartment at their mother's house. She really needed to figure out her life.

Without giving him an opportunity to say anything else, she dropped into her sister's small car and closed her door. She did have somewhere to be. The auto-supply store, for new belts. See? She hadn't even lied.

Those last few minutes with Greyson had just thrown her off her game for some bizarre reason. There was no way she could even ponder any kind of relationship with him other than a professional one.

Plus, he had two kids—and everyone knew she didn't do kids. Kids scared her. They were so easily lost or broken. And Greyson terrified her. He was one of the most closed-off people she had ever met. Well, other than the boyfriend that had lied about his identity.

There was something wrong with her. It was more than being a poor judge of character. People she loved and trusted used her.

McKinsey was too secretive, and she

couldn't trust herself to see the warning flags. God had made them bright yellow and wildly waving in Atlanta, but she'd been having too much fun to pay attention. She had stopped going to church and hadn't once opened her Bible or spent any time in prayer. It was all different now.

God, I'm living in Your presence now and listening to You. I promised that I would be your servant and follow Your word.

She had a plan—and part of that plan was to not get distracted by smooth-talking, good-looking men. She had to focus on her future and set it back on course with God.

McKinsey had hired her and her brother to repair his barn, and that's what they would do. She was learning to lock down her unreliable emotions and get her job done.

Greyson stood at the playroom door and watched the girls sort their toys. He picked up one of the dogs' chew toys and rotated it in his fingers.

The twins had given him a purpose and a reason to live during the darkest days after Jessica's murder. When he hadn't wanted to open his eyes to face another morning without her, they had pulled him out of bed. For them he had pushed through the impotent rage and made sure the man who had gunned down his wife in cold blood would spend the rest of his life behind bars.

For the first year, his anger had even been thrown at God. Now that that rage had settled, he had to find a way back to a normal life for his girls. Jessica had worked to protect all children. It had ended up getting her killed, but she would want him to carry on for the twin gifts they had been given.

No matter how hard he tried, there would be parts of him that were changed forever. The day he met Jessica had changed him. He had become aware of the larger picture, and his life had become bigger than his own wants and desires.

With her giant heart for all those hurting and lost, she had opened his eyes to a huge world that needed love and kindness. She had been a warrior for the weak, and he had been so proud of her.

The day he had witnessed her violent death had put him on a strange new path that didn't include her.

He had lost his confidence. The world was an ugly place, and he didn't know how to protect the people he loved.

It seemed a lifetime ago that he had all the answers. He had been a man in charge of his future, and he was blessed with a woman that was nothing but joy and goodness. He had experienced a love most people never even imagined.

It had started January 24, the first time he saw Jessica in the campus library. In just a few days it would mark twenty-one years ago that she had come into his life. He had asked the pretty girl to get a cup of coffee with him. Two years later, he had asked the brilliant woman to marry him on the same date. Two years to that day, the woman with the biggest and bravest heart he knew had married him. The world had been his.

His fist clenched. The dog toy snapped in half. The day of their eighth wedding anniversary had become the anniversary of her murder. He looked at the broken toy in his hands. His life had gone from beauty to ashes.

He could see it as clearly as if it had happened just a few days ago.

They had gone out to eat and visit a few art galleries so that she could add to her collection. The girls had just turned four, and Jessica was talking about trying again to add on to their family. An old SUV with blacked-out windows had pulled up on the curb. He had pulled Jessica closer to him and made to move around the vehicle when a window had slid down and a man looked straight at them.

Then there were a couple of popping sounds, and Jessica's hand slipped out of his as she fell. The car peeled off. The man had shot Jessica.

He caught her before her head hit the concrete. "Grey?" Her voice was strained. He looked around for someone to help. A woman with a phone ran to them and called 9-1-1.

They'd asked him questions, but he'd focused all his attention on his wife, begging her to stay with him. It was the only time she'd ignored him.

In that moment, his life had been changed forever. He'd lost his wife and had become a key witness in putting a dangerous member of the cartel behind bars for life.

Letting the toy slip to the floor and lowering his forehead into his hands, Greyson closed his eyes and cleared his mind of the terrible images. Her birthday had been last week, but he couldn't celebrate it with the girls. The less they knew, the better.

He hated January.

Jessica wouldn't want him to waste his life with bitterness. It had taken them five years to get pregnant with the twins. They were true gifts, and Jessica had been the most incredible mother.

He had been so busy building their company that she'd made sure they had quality time together when he was home. Being the fun parent was a blessing he had taken for granted. Now it was his responsibility to balance it all.

In the first days of the trial, life had become surreal. To keep them safe, the three of them had taken on new names and moved, cutting all ties to their old life. Now that the trial was over and the man was serving life for Jessica's murder, Greyson wanted to start over, far away from any bad memories or lingering threats.

Because Greyson's testimony was against one member of the cartel specifically, the US Marshals Service felt that they were safe as long as he remained in prison. Since the man had made a direct threat toward the girls, however, they were being extra cautious.

Knowing Greyson's background in landscaping, Diego helped him come up with a new plan for his life. Growing wildflowers for a commercial market in an off-the-map Texas town had sounded like a perfect place for Greyson to raise his daughters. He had to start from scratch without any of his past contacts. He had done it before and loved the challenge of building a new business from the ground, but Jessica had been by his side.

He prayed that leaving everyone they knew behind had been the right decision.

With his first business he had never had a moment of doubt that it would succeed. Doubt was an everyday companion now.

The twins had their heads together. They were looking at something, then jumping back and giggling. He smiled. The days were getting brighter than he had thought possible during the trial. Not every breath hurt.

But today something had happened that left him uncomfortable.

Savannah Espinoza had charmed him in a way no woman had done since the day he'd met Jessica, all those years ago.

Tonight, he promised himself he would start unpacking so the girls didn't grow up thinking paper plates and red plastic cups were the only serving options.

His walls were blank. Not a single throw pillow, blanket or book softened the living space. Jessica would have loved this house, but she would fuss at him for leaving it so plain. It had nothing of her warmth or creativity. The girls deserved more. They deserved better than him as a parent. *God, I don't understand why You left me to raise them alone.*

Jessica had been a better parent, a better person, than he could ever be. Several boxes sat on the kitchen table they had never eaten at. They hadn't been allowed any personal items that would identify them; the only things he had managed to keep were dishes. Everything else was new. He took out a pocketknife and cut the seal on the box closest to him. Pulling back the cardboard flap, he looked inside.

It contained the colorful coffee cups Jessica had gathered from their travels, each one from a local artist. Not ready to go through those, he moved to the next box.

Pulling out something swaddled in paper, he unwrapped it and found the plates they had received as a wedding gift. He put them back and closed the lid. He was exhausted, and if he started this now, he'd be here all night going through each memory.

He'd had to leave her artwork and personal quilts behind with her sister. Maybe he shouldn't have fought for plates and cups, but he had wanted something to share with the girls that had been from their mother.

He turned away from the boxes. Tonight, he didn't have the time or energy. Maybe tomorrow.

It would be paper plates and red cups for lunch today.

He joined the twins in the playroom.

"Daddy, will Ms. Savannah be coming back?" Abilene asked.

"We liked her. She was nice. And she'll help us clean the porch, so you won't have to worry about it," Evelyn told him. Both girls nodded.

Very serious as always, Abilene interlocked her fingers. "We'll pay her. We have nine dollars and thirty-five cents. Do you think that will be enough?"

He sat on the window seat and opened his arms. "Come here." They both ran to him.

"I love you." His voice was a little rough as he hugged them close.

"We're sorry, Daddy."

"I know you were trying to surprise me. That was very nice of you, but from now on, ask me before you use any of my supplies. I would have told you that was a primer for pipes, not paint. Do you need more art supplies?"

They nodded.

"We can set you up in an art area like you had before. I'll get you a table just for drawing and painting. You can help design the mural we're going to paint in the barn. But I need to see your thumbnails first."

"Thank you, Daddy. But why our thumbnails first?" They looked at him in confusion, then at their thumbs.

He chuckled. "Not those thumbnails. The rendering of your ideas. Draw a bunch of sketches, and we'll discuss them and then pick the one that works best. That's what real artists do."

"That sounds fun. Can Ms. Savannah come over and paint with us?" Evelyn was grinning.

Abilene's smile was tentative. "We talked about it. Since the nanny didn't come, can she watch us when you go to work?"

"No. She's a carpenter I hired to work on the barn. It needs to be ready for our first harvest."

"But we like Ms. Savannah." They gave him identical pouts.

Yeah, so did he. And that worried him.

Chapter Three

❧

"One...two...three...lift." Together, she and Reno lifted a beam and put it back in place. They each secured their end, and then Savannah climbed down the scaffolding, swinging to the ground to work on the second piece.

After a week and a half, they were ahead of schedule. It wasn't much, but it was enough that she was happy about the job, and it gave them confidence to submit bids to other projects. Their dad would be proud of the business they were building.

"You know the best thing about being ahead of schedule?" her brother said, interrupting her thoughts. He didn't like silence the way she did. "It gives us room for unexpected problems. These old buildings love to spring surprises—and usually not good ones."

She and Reno worked well together. He understood how she craved getting lost in the process of working with the wood. He could talk and didn't expect her to answer, but he knew she listened. If there was something to add she would, but most of the time she was silent, and he respected that. He also didn't ask her nosy questions like the rest of the family.

The best part? It had been easy to avoid Greyson. He had stopped by each day, but Reno gave him the updates and then shared any changes Greyson wanted with her. It was a very professional relationship. Just like she wanted.

Late at night when she had nothing else to think about, though, she wondered why it was so easy for Greyson to ignore her. But she couldn't ignore the girls and tried to find out how they were doing through her sisters. Sometimes knowing everyone's business in a small town had it perks.

For some reason they were on her mind all the time. Kids were not normally on her radar. They made her nervous. It was all tied to her losing her brother, Reno, when she was a kid herself. She was put in charge of him—and then couldn't find him. They had searched for hours along the beach without finding a hint of where he had gone. It was terrifying. Fearing he was dead had torn her family to pieces. They had found him, but the trauma had stayed with her.

She slammed a hammer onto the nails, counting each blow to break her thought pattern. If she was going to stay focused on her future and be serious about having no more personal relationships for the next few years, then she needed to clear all thoughts of the little family from her mind.

She moved on to the next board and repeated the process.

Out of sight, out of mind should work. She snarled at the barn. It didn't. It was so easy to identify with the girls. She knew how hard it was to lose a parent at that age. Her father had died after a short battle with cancer. How had the girls lost their mother? Was she dead, or just out of their lives for other reasons? Greyson's reaction to any mention of her was tense. That was a warning flag, right? What was he hiding?

"You okay over there?"

"Yes." But she still had her family, home and community. For her, nothing else had changed. Those poor girls had also lost all their friends and familiar places. That had to be devastating.

* * *

The twins had been completely uprooted and were living in a house that bore no evidence of being a home. Had Greyson unpacked yet, or were there still taped-up boxes in every room?

"Hey, Vannie!"

She rolled her eyes and threw a piece of scrap wood at him. That was the horrid nickname he had called her since he could talk. "Don't call me that."

"Then, answer the first time I call you. Aren't you too old to be gathering dust bunnies? I know you like to get in your zone, but you're just standing there. A while ago you were blitzing the boards as if you had a vendetta. Seriously, are you okay?"

"Fine." She picked up a drill and looked for the next area to attack. She hated that she was giving a man she didn't know so much of her thoughts. And Reno was pushing her. Her little brother was supposed to be the one who gave her space and didn't ask questions. Before she could reply, her phone rang. Putting down the drill, she pulled her phone from her back pocket.

"It's Greyson." Her heart hit the next beat harder. Strange. He usually contacted Reno. Her brother raised a brow.

She answered. "Hello, Mr. McKinsey."

"Thank you for answering, Savannah. I know you're busy." His voice sounded rushed and a little out of breath. "I'm in Houston. The plan was to be back in town to pick up the girls, but well, you know how plans go. The school called. Apparently, the girls were in some sort of altercation that resulted in Abilene's hair being cut and Evelyn hitting someone. The twins are upset, they're suspended, and the school wants me to pick them up now. But like I said, I'm in Houston."

He paused. She heard a door opening and shutting.

"What about the new nanny?" Panic at the thought of picking up the girls at school rattled her.

"You haven't heard? She quit yesterday morning. One day's notice. All she said was she's more of a city girl and didn't realize she would be miles past the middle of nowhere. She thought living close to the beach would be more fun." He chuckled. "I know you say you're not a nanny, but right now you are the only one I know and trust."

She looked over at Reno. "I can call my sister to see if she can do it."

"They don't know your sister, and I'm... Please. They've been asking about you." His voice was flat and hollow. "I'm sorry, but I really need this favor. Honestly, it's a really bad day for several reasons."

But he wasn't going to tell her the reasons, was he? She could imagine him running his fingers through his hair in frustration. "Okay. I'll get them. We're at a good stopping point for now. Reno can easily get the rest done by himself this afternoon."

There was a rush of air. "Thank you. I canceled my last meeting, and I'm heading that way, but I'm two hours out if the traffic is clear. I think you picking them up could make them feel better. They need something to be happy about today."

That delighted her more than it should have. "Is there anything I need to know? Are they okay?"

"I'm not sure. The principal and counselor want to talk to me before the girls go back to school. I'm worried. I need to be there." He grunted. There was a long pause.

"Greyson?"

"I've been out of sorts lately, and they might have picked up on that. This is a tough month, but today is a hard day for me. I tend to get hyper focused on work to avoid it. They're smart." He blew out a long puff of air.

"They needed me today, and I had checked out. I should have been there for them."

"No parent can be everywhere all the time. Is there anything else I should know about their mother? I don't want to say the wrong thing." She was afraid to ask if it was the anniversary of her death. Maybe it was their wedding or her birthday.

There was a silence that stretched out. She wasn't sure he was going to reply.

He sighed. "Their mother passed away. In an accident. It's been tough. They're so smart." It sounded like he hit the steering wheel.

"Um, is it her birthday or something?" She closed her eyes. Please let it be that and not something worse. "If so, I can help the girls with that if it's too hard for you. It was for my mom."

His end of the line remained silent. He wasn't going to tell her. Writing out a note to Reno, she pointed to her truck. He nodded and went back to work. "Greyson? Are you still there?"

"Yeah."

"Okay. I'm on my way to school now. Don't worry about them. The girls will be here when you get home."

A car started. "Thank you, Savannah. This

means a great deal to me. Will you tell the girls it's their mother's birthday? I don't know if I can." The words were hoarse, like he'd been yelling all four quarters at a football game.

"Not a problem. You drive safe. The girls will be okay." They disconnected.

"Savannah?" Pausing at the truck, she turned to find her brother close behind her.

"Greyson's having nanny issues again, and the girls have gotten into some sort of trouble at school. I'm going to go pick them up and watch them until he gets back."

"You? Be careful."

She knew he wasn't talking about the drive to town. "Hey, we worked through lunch. I'll pick something up and bring it back here. We can have a picnic with the girls. It's their mother's birthday."

He nodded, concern still in his soft brown eyes. "I'll finish up this part. It's a one-person job, anyway."

"Okay." Heading into town, Savannah suddenly found it hard to breathe. That was ridiculous. This was no big deal. For her, anyway. But she had a feeling it was for the girls. Their mother was dead, and their nanny had walked out on them the day before her birthday.

Savannah had lashed out a few times at

school, too, not understanding the anger and frustration that boiled inside after her father's death. How long ago had these girls lost their mother?

It didn't take long to get to the school. The front-office staff were dying of curiosity, but they were too polite to ask why she was picking up the McKinsey twins. She had never even picked up her own nieces and nephews. They might be doubting Greyson's judgment in allowing her to be the emergency pickup.

With the girls secured in the bench back seat, she swung by the Painted Dolphin to pick up the lunch she had ordered. A young girl she didn't recognize brought it out with a smile.

Back on the road, she gave the girls her full attention. Abilene's eyes were red. It was obvious she'd been crying, and there was a chunk of hair missing from the left side of her head. A very noticeable chunk.

"Did you want a new hairstyle?"

Evelyn spoke up first. "Caty's hair was on Abilene's desk. It was an accident. She didn't mean to cut her hair. She said she was sorry, but Caty was so mad. She said Abilene did it to be mean, then she grabbed Abby's hair and cut it. I told her to stop and that she had apologized, but she was going to cut it again, so I hit her. She was making my sister cry. The teacher started yelling and called for the principal. She said we were fighting. But we weren't, it was an accident. Right, Abby?"

The other twin nodded. "I didn't see her hair."

"Daddy's going to be so mad at me for hitting her. He says we have to use our words and never hit."

"But I did use my words, and she still cut my hair."

"Your dad will work it out. Who's your teacher?"

"Ms. Nichols," they said at the same time. Savannah knew Beth. Maybe she could talk to her and let her know what the girls were going through.

"Did you get to eat lunch?"

They shook their heads. "We're not hungry." Abilene pouted and crossed her arms.

"Well, I happen to have the best mac and cheese you will ever eat right here in the truck. Along with some chicken tenders and green beans. It could all be yours with a simple please-and-thank-you." She turned into the farm's driveway. "My brother, Reno, is waiting at the barn. We can have a picnic. Your dad's driving in from Houston and should be here in less than two hours."

Both girls brightened. "A picnic? We haven't had one of those since…" Evelyn looked terrified.

"It's okay if you want to talk about your mom with me."

Abilene looked at Evelyn. Panic filled her eyes.

"Daddy doesn't want us to talk about the things that happened before we moved here. This is a new start." She was obviously quoting her father.

"It's okay. Just know that if you want to, you can talk to me, and I'll keep it to myself. I won't even tell my brother. Want to help me carry the food to the barn?"

Evelyn nodded. "We're good helpers." For the first time, excitement lit their eyes. "After our picnic, can we help you work in the barn?"

"Let's eat lunch first, then we'll talk about working."

Evelyn clapped. "Can we go to the house and get Bliss and Finn? They always make us feel better."

"That's a great idea." At the house, she called Reno and told him they would be there soon. She followed the girls through the living room and was sad to see her earlier question answered.

The boxes were in the exact same spot as the last time. The playroom warmed her heart, though. It was organized, but it was undoubtedly a space designed for kids to play and grow. An art table had been added, and there were several pictures scattered among the art supplies and colorful drawings.

The puppies were overly excited to see them.

"Make sure to get their leashes. We don't want to lose them on the farm."

Less than ten minutes later, they were pulling up to the barn. Reno was at the door, hands on his hips and a smile on his face. He was still such a big kid. She had a tough time imagining him as a real firefighter.

The girls and dogs ran to him like a long-lost friend. "So happy y'all could join us." He greeted them with a huge grin.

"Savannah said we can help, and she said she has the best macaroni cheese in the world, and she let us get Finn and Bliss."

The pair of spaniels danced between the girls and Reno. He had a special touch with animals. She'd always thought he could be a veterinarian, but he said the coursework would take away from the fun in life. After one year in college, he had dropped out. One of these days he would grow up. Maybe.

He smiled as he picked up Bliss and rubbed Evelyn's hair. "I set up a picnic table in the barn."

"Yay!" The girls jumped up and down, exciting the puppies even more.

Reno went to the truck and helped Savannah and the girls with the food.

"It smells so good. Better than the cafeteria food." Evelyn carried one of the bags inside.

It didn't take them long to devour the lunch, then they started exploring the main area of the barn. Watching them closely, Savannah started packing the extra food away.

Reno grabbed the container with the macaroni and cheese. "You're not putting this up. I'm eating it."

"I was gonna save it for leftovers."

"Too bad, so sad." He shoveled another spoonful into his mouth. "There won't be any leftovers, so you'll have to eat Mom's cooking tonight. Poor baby," he said around another mouthful of her favorite mac and cheese.

"Eat the green beans too," she said. His eating habits were so bad. "You eat like a four-year-old."

"Green beans? One afternoon of playing nanny and you're pushing better eating habits on me. You're more like our mom and sisters than you're willing to admit."

"Nanny?" The thought horrified her. "Everyone knows I'm not good with kids." She gave him her best glare, but he just grinned and took the last bit of the creamy macaroni.

"Driving kids around. Feeding them. Watching them until their dad comes home. Nanny." He knew her buttons too well.

She stifled the urge to stick her tongue out. Instead, she settled for saying, "You're ridiculous."

The girls ran up to them, Finn and Bliss right on their heels. "Can we help fix the barn?"

"Sure," Reno agreed.

"No," she made her voice louder than his. Her glares had stopped working on him. He led the twins to one of the work areas with power tools. Greyson wouldn't like that. "It could be dangerous." She followed.

"We can help. We'll be careful." Their words tumbled out on top of each other as they batted their big eyes at Reno.

It was over. He nodded. "A little sanding wouldn't hurt anyone." He took the girls to some of the beams laid out on sawhorses and put them to work with sheets of sandpaper. They loved it.

"See." He grinned at Savannah. "No tools, but they get to feel the pride of helping their dad refurbish this beautiful barn and build the family business. They'll learn to love wood-working like you did with Dad."

She went back to work, but she didn't get much done. Reno was impulsive, and he was always ready to play without always thinking through the consequences.

But he was right. Working with the girls and showing them how to find the beauty in the wood brought back some of her favorite memories of going to work with her dad.

Finishing her cuts, she went over to check on the girls' work. "Nicely done. Now whenever you come into the barn, you'll know you had a hand in restoring it."

Abilene was right next to Savannah, and she slipped her small hand into hers. It was so soft compared to her calloused ones.

"Thank you for coming to get us," Abilene whispered. "It's been a very bad day, but you've made it better."

And with that, all her insides melted to goo. *"De nada, mija."*

"That means *It's nothing, my girl child*."

Savannah laughed. "That is a very literal translation. It's a way to say *you're welcome*. You speak Spanish?"

"We were in a dual program at our old

school. This one doesn't do that." A sad frown marred the sweet little face.

"I can teach you," she said and leaned down to whisper, "but don't listen to Reno's Spanish. His is *no bueno*."

"I heard that!" her brother yelled with overly dramatic hurt feelings. "My Spanish is *mucho grande*."

She rolled her eyes. "That doesn't even make sense, proving my point."

With a tentative smile, Abilene giggled, then ran to her sister.

Reno nudged her with his elbow. "I hate to be the one to give you the shocking news, but you're good with kids. Especially those girls."

She elbowed him back. "I didn't ask for your opinion." The idea of being responsible for a child scared her more than anything else.

With a charming lopsided smile, he winked, then went back to work. "You know what happened in Atlanta wasn't your fault. You've been around kids your whole life. You practically raised me, and I turned out okay."

"Did you? Jury's still out on that one." They had come so close to losing him because of her. "You know I was the one watching you when you disappeared for sixteen hours. And with Colin and my art group, I was too naive. Looking back, I can see all the warning signs, but I never questioned them. I thought it would make me disloyal."

The memory burned her throat, and her stupid eyes built up tears. She looked down to get them back under control before he saw them.

His arm was around her. "Hey. That was a long time ago, and you were just a kid. No one blamed you for me sneaking into the boat to hide. I'm sure Margarita was in charge. And those losers in Atlanta took advantage of your loyalty."

He didn't get it. "Thanks, but you were too young to remember. I was in charge of you. Mom and Daddy were both furious and terrified. I had one job that day. To watch you. We thought… You were gone all day with no trace. It was horrible. Everyone kept asking me where I saw you last." She closed her eyes as the helpless feelings washed over her. This was not helping, and all it would do was make Reno feel guilty. It hadn't been his fault. He had only been four.

He put his arm around her and pulled her in for a giant hug. "You're right. I don't remember any of it, but I remember the grand adventure sneaking away in a boat. I'm so sorry you were going through that. I'm fine. Please. Let it go."

Taking a deep breath, she opened her eyes and smiled at him. "You're right. It was a long time ago. Get back to work." Patting his chest, she stepped back and looked for the girls. They weren't in the barn.

A paralyzing fear seized her heart. They were gone.

"Reno? Where are they?" Sweat broke out over her entire body.

"It's okay. They're here somewhere. Evelyn, Abilene," he called out.

The side door was open. She ran. At the threshold, all the tension left her body, and she sagged against the frame. The girls were playing at the concrete water trough. Their laughter was so bright it made the air lighter and the day sparkle.

Evelyn threw a ball of mud at her sister, hitting her smack in the chest. Abilene screamed, then put her thumb over the end of the hose to squirt her sister with a blast of water. The dogs jumped, snapping at the stream of water, trying to catch it. Greyson was going to kill her.

"Girls! What are you doing?"

All four froze and, in slow motion, turned to her. Evelyn stood on one end of the rectangle tank opposite Abilene. A new ball of mud oozed through her fingers. Wide-eyed, she sat down suddenly on the thick wall of the trough as if she didn't have a care in the world. She thrust her hand behind her back—as if Savannah wouldn't see her muddy weapon.

"Finn was thirsty." Her voice was pitchy.

Both girls were completely covered in mud. As were the puppies. Oh, the puppies!

There was so much mud that she didn't know which was Finn and which was Bliss. The girls' laughter was gone, and they hid their gazes from her, staring at the ground. They looked more serious than when she had picked them up from school.

They had been so sad and distraught, her heart had broken for them. The laughter she had just heard was nothing but joy. Until she'd walked out and yelled at them.

Abilene held the water hose behind her. The water was still running, and it pooled at her feet, making an even bigger mud hole.

Evelyn tried to pick up one of the puppies, but the little dog wiggled and slipped down into the mud again, rolling.

"You didn't tell me you were leaving the barn." Her mind was whirling. What was she going to do? She moved closer to Abilene and turned off the water. Now mud caked her boots. The little girl's shoulders were trembling. Her head was down. Was she crying? Savannah put a hand on her shoulder and, without thinking, pulled the girl close.

Oh, that was a mistake. Now she had mud on her. But at least the water had stopped.

One of the puppies shook its coat, finishing with its undocked tail. Chunks of mud went flying, spraying her and Abilene.

Evelyn giggled, then covered her mouth, her eyes wide with mortification. She rushed to the dog and tried to pick it up. "She didn't mean it. We're sorry."

Abilene nodded. "Please don't get mad. It was my fault. I tried to wash the mud off Finn, then Bliss got in and swam around. We slipped trying to get her out, then we all had mud on us. I accidentally sprayed Evelyn, and then I fell, and I was in the mud and Evelyn sprayed me and… And, and then…" She started crying in earnest.

"We're sorry." Evelyn was hugging her sister now, and the pups jumped up on them.

Reno came out and started laughing. "I see you found them. Seriously, Savannah. Leave it to you to find a way to cover the kids you're in charge of in mud from head to foot."

"You think it's funny?" She scraped off a glob of mud that clung to her overalls and threw it at him. He ducked, and it hit the barn wall.

"Oh no, you didn't." He stalked her. Retribution burned in his eyes.

She backed up. "No. I missed. I'm standing with the children."

He didn't slow down.

It was a battle. "Girls. We have to stop him. On the count of three, throw your best mud ball."

"Oh no, you don't." Reno scooped up a handful of mud.

"Now… Three… Three." The laughter was back as the girls helped her attack Reno with the mud. The dogs jumped and barked, loving the renewed game. Her team had horrible aim. One part of a mud ball found Reno, then he went for the water hose. He was still mostly clean.

When the car came up behind them, they all turned. Savannah's stomach fell to the bottom of her feet. It was Greyson. She placed her hand on each of the girls' shoulders.

"Oh no. It's Daddy."

"He's going to be so mad about everything."

"We're never going to get to play again." Even the pups whined and cowered behind her.

"Don't worry. I'll explain this is my fault."

"This should be interesting." Reno dropped the hose and crossed his arms, leaning against the side of the pump house.

"Not helping," she said between clenched teeth. There had to be a way to make this good for the girls and Greyson. It was a hard day for them all.

They all stood in silence waiting for Greyson to join them.

Chapter Four

Greyson slowed. From the first day they'd brought the girls home, he had always been able to tell them apart. Right now, he couldn't point to Abilene with confidence. How had they gotten so much mud over everything?

First, he couldn't fathom his sweet girls getting in a fight at school today. Now this?

What was he doing wrong? Was it the stress of being in the witness protection program? There were so many rules, and the girls were too young to understand, so now their childhood was coated in lies and false memories. Had he made a mistake testifying?

But he couldn't have lived with himself if the man had walked. And there had been the threat to the girls' lives. The knot that now resided in his gut tightened. He would find a way for them to have a childhood.

When he had driven up the road, they had been having too much fun to even notice his approach. He didn't remember the last time they had lost themselves in playing and laughter. But as soon as they saw him, everyone froze. His arrival had sucked all the joy out of the room...or barn. He should scold them, but they looked so scared—of him. All of them, including Savannah. He shouldn't have called her. She was getting too close to the girls. That was how secrets were exposed. But he couldn't keep them isolated. There should be people in their lives other than him. But every time they interacted it was a risk.

They also had a sadness that hurt him.

With a deep breath he imagined what Jessica would do in this situation. His response needed to be intentional. That meant not yelling and screaming as every fiber of his being was inclined to do.

It was a difficult day that had just kept getting worse. He had enough self-awareness to know that most of this frustration had nothing to do with the girls. If he could just get them through January... And now he had turned their anniversary day into her birthday.

But was it too much to ask for just one day to go as planned? He had wanted to pick up the girls from school, grab dinner to take home and curl up on the couch with them to watch some happy, sing-along movie. Something that had nothing to do with a dead parent.

He should know by now not to expect any easy days that went according to plan. But this behavior needed some sort of response. First, they were in trouble at school, and now they were fighting in the mud.

This was a major cleanup job that could take hours. And in the rush to get to the girls, he hadn't stopped to get dinner. That was the least of his problems now.

He stood in front of them, trying to figure out where to start. Silence surrounded them, until a thick glob of mud fell off someone and hit the water. The girls lost the battle to stifle nervous giggles.

A frustrated growl escaped him before he could stop it, and Savannah's eyes went wide. Despite the fear in her gaze, she stepped forward, as if to shield the girls from him.

All giggling stopped. He moved his gaze from Reno to Savannah. Her brother was leaning against the pump house with his arms crossed, smirking as if he knew his sister was going to get in trouble. Making eye contact, the younger man straightened, his expression going serious. "Sorry about the mess. We—"

"We're finished in the barn for the day." Savannah cut her little brother off. "Reno was putting everything away when all this started." She turned to Reno. "Go ahead and clean up the workspace. Don't you have a firehouse meeting tonight?"

Reno shook his head. "*Cabeza de toro*," he said to Savannah.

He called her a bull? Greyson wasn't sure what *cabeza* meant. *Head*, maybe? *Head of the bull?* He grinned. Her brother had called her bullheaded.

Reno turned to Greyson. "If you need anything, let me know. *El jefe*—" he tilted his head to Savannah "—has given me my orders." The slang for *boss* sounded a little sarcastic.

As Reno disappeared into the barn, Greyson's gaze went back to Savannah. She probably didn't even realize she was trying to protect everyone from him, even her six-foot-three brother. Mud covered her left cheek and ran down the side of her neck. There were smeared paw prints across her pink overalls and grimy flecks in her braided hair. And she was soaked.

But she held her chin up as she looked directly at him.

He slid his hands into his pockets as he thought out each word.

Calling the twins *inquisitive* had been an understatement, but when they realized they had done something wrong, they usually worked hard to make it right. They didn't like people being upset with them.

His girls had moved close to each other, hugging the muddy pups. The stuff was caked on so thick, he couldn't even tell the color of the dogs.

"We have a lot to discuss today. Let's start with this." He waved at the mess. "Explain to me why everything and everyone is covered in mud."

Savannah moved between the girls and pulled them to her sides. "Yes. It has been an incredibly stressful day for everyone. After we ate, we came out to give the dogs a drink. Bliss and Finn jumped into the tank. In the process of getting them out, the girls got muddy. In Texas, we might not have snowball fights, but we do love a good mud-ball battle." She was looking at the girls.

After a few beats of silence, she raised her head and met his gaze. Despite her lifted chin daring him to say a harsh word, her face also wore a tentative look.

With a squeeze of his daughters' small shoulders, she stepped forward. "I'll help clean everything."

He raised an eyebrow, then scanned the area. Every square inch was covered. How would they even begin? There was no way the girls or dogs could get in a car.

Reno came in from behind him. "I always have towels in my truck and blankets in case of an emergency. I'll stack them over here." He set them down against the barn. "Are you sure you don't need my help?" He looked at his sister.

"No. Go to your meeting. We've got this covered. Could you bring the leashes out? We left them in the barn."

Savannah lifted the girls to stand on the concrete edge of the trough. The low wall was about a foot wide, so the girls had no problem balancing. "We'll wash the bulk of the mud off here."

Greyson went to help, but she held up her hand, then pointed to his shoes. "Those look like leather, the expensive kind. I've got this."

Reno stood next to him. "Here are the leashes and a pair of mud boots. Thought they would come in handy."

Greyson thanked him, then balancing on one leg, he took off his dress shoes and slipped on the boots. They ended right under his knees. Greyson didn't consider himself short at five foot ten, but he felt like a kid in his dad's boots. "Thanks."

"Have fun." With a parting smirk, Reno left. Greyson went over to the dogs and put their leashes on. The mud squished under the boots.

Savannah stopped him. "Just toss the leashes. You shouldn't come any closer." Her gaze scanned him up and down. "That suit looks just as nice as those shoes." She turned her focus back on the girls and their muddy pets. She caught the leashes and gave them to the girls, then starting with their hair, she washed most of the big chunks off the girls and dogs.

"It's cold," Evelyn squealed as Savannah washed off their heads.

Greyson narrowed his gaze. Was half of her hair gone? "It's the same water you were just playing in."

"We'll get the majority of the mud out of your hair and your clothes before we go to the house. Then it's nice warm showers for everyone." Savannah looked over at him. "Once we get most of the mud off, they can ride in the back of my truck to the house for their detailing. No need to ruin a good suit or your car."

"The suit can be cleaned but thank you for the use of your truck." This day was not getting any better. Leaving them, he took off his jacket, placed it with his shoes in the car and rolled up his sleeves.

Back in the muddy area, he took the squirming puppy from Abilene. "I'll dunk the dogs and wrap them in the towel." After doing so, he secured both dogs in the bed of Savannah's Silverado truck. Even covered in towels and blankets, they looked miserable.

"Abilene's done," Savannah called.

He grabbed another towel and patted her down, then put her in the back with the dogs.

"Thank you, Daddy."

"You're welcome. Now, tell me why the school called me to pick you up early. What happened?" He eyed her hair. This was not going to be good.

"I'm sorry, Daddy."

"It wasn't her fault," Evelyn hollered and stomped her foot from the concrete stock tank.

Frustrated, he turned to Evelyn. "That is not how you talk to people."

Savannah had turned the water hose on herself. Turning off the water, she wrapped

Evelyn in a blanket and carried her to the truck. "Just explain what happened." She caressed Evelyn's wet hair.

With a frown, his outspoken daughter nodded. "Sorry for yelling, Daddy. I was so mad. Caty cut Abilene's hair, but we got in trouble." She pointed to her sister's hair. It was a good ten inches shorter on one side.

He ran both of his hands through his hair and pushed his fingers against his scalp. With a deep breath, he looked at Evelyn. "So out of nowhere without any provocation, this little girl cut your sister's hair. I was told Abilene cut Caty's hair first." That had confused him. It didn't sound like something the younger twin would ever do.

"That's a lie." Evelyn looked at the sky before cutting her gaze to Abilene. "Well…"

Huddled in the blanket, Abilene had big tears in her eyes. "It was an accident. I didn't mean to."

Evelyn stood in the truck bed now. "It was a little bitty piece. She wouldn't even have known it had been cut if she hadn't seen it on the desk." She went over every detail in one long sentence. When she paused for a breath, Abilene jumped in.

"I used my words, Daddy. I asked her to

please stop. Her hair was getting in the way. I was just trying to do my work."

"Abby did say she was sorry. But then Caty said the *s*-word and grabbed a whole bunch of Abby's hair."

"The *s*-word?" Savannah looked horrified, but Greyson suspected it wasn't as bad as it sounded.

Evelyn nodded and leaned toward Savannah. "*Shut up*," she whispered. "I told her to stop. But she reached over and cut Abby's hair. She threw it to the ground and started grabbing more. I shoved her away, and she fell. Then hollered like a baby. Ms. Nichols ran over."

He rubbed his forefinger and his thumb over the bridge of his nose and prayed for patience and wisdom. He was in short supply of both. He looked back at the girls.

Evelyn snuggled in next to Abilene, who was softly crying. Her wet hair hung long on one side but curled above her ear on the other. He'd have to find someone to even it out.

Breathing was a good plan. "It sounds as if it escalated very quickly. Is there something you could've done early in the situation so that it didn't get to the point of cutting hair, yelling and crying? Pushing and hitting are unacceptable, Evelyn."

"I know, Daddy. Abilene tried to use her words, but it didn't work. Caty wouldn't stop."

"There's another solution that you didn't try. Can you think of it?"

They shook their heads, then looked at Savannah. She twisted her lips as if in deep thought. "Did you ask Ms. Nichols for help?"

Evelyn gasped and shook her head. "Daddy, we can't be tattletales and snitches. We would never have friends."

He sighed. "You don't have to tell Ms. Nichols that Caty is bothering you. You just need to tell Ms. Nichols that you're having a rough time getting your work done. Tonight, you will write an apology to Caty for the aggressive behavior and to Ms. Nichols for disrupting her class."

Evelyn sat up. "To Caty?" Outrage tainted her sweet voice. "She hurt Abby. Then she lied. She cried big fat tears and she told Ms. Nichols and Ms. Abernathy that we said mean things to her, then cut her hair. We didn't. We're the only ones that got in trouble, but Caty started it. It's not fair."

"She didn't get in trouble at all?" He clenched his jaw. Why wouldn't the other girl be in trouble too? He needed to talk with Ms. Abernathy and get this straightened out before he made any judgments.

At a loss as to what to do, he gripped the back of the truck and looked at the mud on the rubber boots Reno had lent him. He had let his girls down. They had needed him today, and he was too deep in his own funk to protect them.

He had moved them to Texas to make a better life, but that wasn't working out as planned either. They weren't adjusting at all.

A hand touched his shoulder. He looked up and found Savannah, her eyes full of compassion. That just about did him in. The burden of being in witness protection sat heavier on his shoulders than ever before. He wanted to tell her everything and ask her what he should do for the girls. But he couldn't.

There was a new pounding in his head. His gaze moved away from her and landed on the barn. He took a moment to refocus.

"Daddy, we're sorry. We didn't mean to make you more sad."

Now he had the guilt of his daughter worrying about taking care of him. That wasn't right. "Why do you think I'm sad?"

They looked at each other before turning back to him. Evelyn spoke. "We don't want you to be sad about Mommy, but we know we aren't supposed to talk about her either."

The silence was heavy. He reached over

and hugged the girls. Then he stepped back and wiped at his eyes. "I never meant that you couldn't talk to me about your mother. Losing her does make me sad, but remembering her also makes me happy. I loved your mother. You were her greatest joys. You can always talk to me about her. I just don't want other people in our business." How had he messed this up so much?

"Ms. Savannah said we can talk to her, and she won't tell anyone," Abilene said.

"Not even her brother," Evelyn added. "Would that be okay?"

He pulled them close. This was the problem of having people in their lives. Things could slip. "I love you both so much. We'll talk about it later." They were getting closer to Savannah, and he wasn't sure how to handle it.

The woman in his thoughts clapped her hands. "Why don't we get the girls home and into clean, dry clothes. Tomorrow, you can talk to Ms. Nichols and Mrs. Abernathy. We'll get this all straightened out. Let's put them in the back seat. You can come with us and get your car later. After you get the mud off you." She smiled.

He needed that smile. "They're soaked. Are you sure you want them in your truck?"

"Wet kids are nothing. Believe me, it's seen worse. Come on, let's get you home."

Home. That did sound good. With some of the weight off his shoulders, he lifted Abilene out of the truck. They both pouted. "But we want to ride in the back of the truck!" Evelyn cried.

"That's what farm kids do. Did you when you visited as a kid?"

He opened his mouth to say no, but Savannah put her hand on his arm and saved him. His story was he had grown up on a farm.

She smiled at him. A smile that did some very strange things to the mixed-up feelings he already had today.

"It's just to the house. You can ride with them. It's fun to feel the wind in your hair for short trips." Her expression softened. "So I hear today is your mom's birthday. Big days like this can be hard for everyone when the people we love aren't with us any longer. How about I drive slow and y'all can think of a way to celebrate her memory."

The girls went still, their eyes going wide as they stared at their father. They looked terrified to move. Were they still afraid to upset him? His heart twisted.

"Is today Mommy's birthday?"

It wasn't, but they weren't allowed to celebrate the real date. So today would no longer be their wedding anniversary or the anniversary of her death. Today would become her birthday. One day he would be able to tell the girls the truth. He hoped.

He could be so selfish sometimes. With what he tried for a reassuring smile, he put Abilene in the truck bed and climbed in with them.

"Remember, I said you can talk to me about your mom at any time. Planning something in her memory sounds like a great idea to me."

With huge smiles, they scooted apart to make room for him. Savannah took out her phone. "I'll take a picture."

"No. No pictures." That was probably too short. "I mean…"

"I can take it with your phone," she offered.

He pulled his phone out and handed it to her. "Thank you."

"De nada." She clicked on the phone, smiled at the girls and got into the truck.

Did she know that his gratitude was for more than the picture?

Chapter Five

With the precious cargo in the bed of her truck, Savannah drove slowly enough to miss any washed-out ruts in the dirt road. It also gave her the time she needed to get the unruly teenage girl inside her under control.

That overly excited girl had fallen in love way too quickly, too many times and for stupid reasons. Some would say she had Daddy issues because she'd lost her father so young, but that seemed to be an easy cop-out. She was loved by her family. She had two brothers that she adored. It was just poor judgment on her part.

The last time she'd felt this giddy, it had all been a lie. Her first time out on her own. She had felt so grown-up in Atlanta. She had cool artist friends in a trendy downtown loft and a boyfriend who seemed perfect.

She had floated when she walked. Her life was everything she had dreamed it would be. But dreams are illusions, and it's hard to wake up from them. She had been devastated at her foolishness when she'd learned the truth about Colin.

There was no way she could trust this feeling. She had promised God that she would be happily single and emotionally free as she focused on Him and the business with her brother. Greyson had made her think about her art too.

Creating new pieces of art to center her was a part of who she was, and she shouldn't let Colin/James take that spark from her.

But when Greyson had walked up in that suit, all clean-shaven with his hair combed back… At that memory, her grip tightened around the steering wheel.

He'd looked like he was on a photo shoot for some fancy fashion magazine. A herd of butterflies had broken from their cocoons and taken flight somewhere in her chest. Which was weird, because his look had never been her type.

She had always been drawn to the edgy, tortured artist. Like the person Colin had pretended to be. She snorted and shook her head.

Yeah, that had never worked out well for her. Her psyche was overcompensating.

Greyson was a farmer and a single dad who was still grieving his wife. He had no business looking that good—and she had no business noticing.

Parking in front of the house, she glanced into the rearview mirror. Greyson was standing, Finn and Bliss circling him in excitement. The girls were giggling as he unsuccessfully tried to free his legs from their leashes.

Getting out, she leaned against the back of her truck. "Need some help?"

"Nooo." Sarcasm dripped. "Not at all. I'm good." He tried to get one leg out of the web of nylon leashes and almost lost his balance.

She might have giggled with the girls.

Abilene unleashed Finn while Evelyn tried to detangle Bliss by pushing her back around. The excited pup wiggled in her arms, both tails wagging with the power of turbines.

The girls lost all control and went into full-belly laughter again. Greyson grinned as he unwrapped Finn's leash from his legs, and long dimples she hadn't seen before made an appearance. This little family lit her heart.

Bliss wiggled free from Evelyn and ran to the edge of the truck, licking Savannah's face. Picking the puppy up, she held her free hand out. "Give me her leash and help your dad get free of Finn."

It didn't take long to get everyone straightened out and on the porch.

"Daddy, we want to show Savannah our room."

"I'm sure she has somewhere else to be. Her workday has long since ended."

He opened the door, then stood back to allow everyone in the foyer. The boxes were still stacked against the walls. There weren't just regular moving boxes either. Most of them had shipping labels. Like it was all brand-new merchandise.

Up close, the shadows under his eyes announced how physically tired he was. She knew from firsthand experience that it was mental exhaustion that hit the hardest.

She wasn't a single parent with an overwhelming amount of responsibility. She couldn't even handle owning a pet. But as she grew older, she often wondered how her mother had held it together after the death of her father. How had she filled their house with so much joy and love while she had to be grieving and lost?

Did she dare ask if they wanted to do something for their mother's birthday?

She reached out and touched his upper arm.

"How about I take them upstairs to finish cleaning up? Then they can show me their room and get nice clean pajamas on. Do you have something in the freezer that will be easy to throw in the oven?"

"Daddy said we could make brownies and put ice cream on top." Abilene wrinkled her nose and narrowed her eyes. "It was Mommy's favorite, right?" Both girls looked at him.

"Yes." He pulled them close. He swallowed a couple of times before plastering on a stiff smile. "She would let you help her make it, but you ended up with more mix on your faces than in the pan."

The girls giggled.

Evelyn twisted to look up at him. "Call someone to bring dinner to the house, Daddy."

His chuckle was dry. "Sweetheart, we don't live in town anymore. There are no delivery services that drive this far out."

"Then, what are we going to do for Mommy's birthday?" Both girls look horrified.

"First, you'll get cleaned up and ready for bed. You can wear your pj's to dinner. I'm fairly certain there are frozen pizzas and a brownie mix."

The girls cheered.

Savannah pushed Abilene's lopsided curls

back. "Start the brownie mix. Don't worry about dinner. Once we get the mud monsters cleaned up, we'll have a dinner extravaganza! It's my favorite kind of dinner."

Eyes wide, the twins turned to her. "What's that?"

Savannah put her hands on her hips. "Making dinner without cooking is my superpower. We'll have a scavenger hunt in the kitchen and find the most interesting food that doesn't have to be cooked. Then we'll see what everyone else found and plate it all together."

The girls jumped up and down and clapped. "Yay! Daddy, you go find what you think is interesting and keep it a secret. We'll get ready, then come down and help with the brownies. Can we eat at the table with candles? Would Mommy like that?" Eyes big and uncertain, they turned to their father for confirmation. Her heart broke for them.

"Yep." Greyson blinked, looking lost for a moment. "Your mother loved having a candlelit dinner for any and every occasion she could think of." His lips tightened for a second. "Sometimes just because it was Tuesday, and Tuesday needed to be celebrated also. She said life was too short not to make every day special."

Oh no. He looked as if he was about to

cry. That would not be the mood he'd want
to set for the girls. They'd be afraid of talking
about their mother ever again if they thought
he was sad. She jumped in front of him and
held out her hands for the girls to take. "So,
a candlelit-dinner-table extravaganza sounds
like a perfect thing to do tonight in honor of
your mother's memory." He never mentioned
his wife by name. Was it too painful or was
he hiding something?

"Yes, an extravaganza dinner surprise!
That's a fun birthday idea for Mommy."
Abilene took hold of her hand, then grabbed
her sister. "We need to hurry. Don't waste
time, Daddy."

Savannah saw the corner of his mouth
twitch. With that one little suppressed grin,
she stood taller. Bringing any joy to this man
was an accomplishment that made her proud.

He nodded. "Challenge accepted."

"Come on, Savannah." They took off up
the stairs ahead of her, the dogs running
alongside. A wet trail followed them.

She paused for a moment and made eye
contact with him. "I'll clean this up when I'm
done with the girls. Take a minute to relax.
We'll be busy for a little bit. When we come
down, I'll take care of dinner."

Now, why did she offer to take care of dinner? She couldn't boil eggs. She twisted her mouth and tilted her head to the ceiling. "But don't expect anything great. My mom and sisters are all incredible cooks, even my brothers outdo me in the kitchen. But I've survived, so unless you're super meticulous, just relax. I can't cook a fancy dinner, but I know how to have fun and get us fed."

His whole expression softened as he looked at her. "It's been a long time since I had anyone tag-team with the girls. Thank you. I really appreciate it."

"Savannah!" both girls called from the top of the stairs, and the dogs barked.

"I'm coming." With a wink to reassure him, she went up the stairs. The bathroom was between two bedrooms, but the girls shared one of them. The other held more unpacked boxes.

While the girls showered, she washed the last of the grime off Finn and Bliss in the sink. The girls said they washed them once a week.

It was so much easier to care for smaller dogs than the huge dogs her brothers loved.

Savannah smiled as she listened to the girls. They helped wash each other off and made plans, talking about the things their mother liked. Some of it sounded as if it was from a fairy tale. They had been so young, and Greyson didn't seem to talk about it, so they probably were filling in holes to make their mother real for them.

Once they were clean, she took the blow-dryer to the dogs. To her surprise, they loved it. Both stood noses up and eyes closed, as if the warm air was the best thing in the world. She laughed. "You're little divas." They stood on the counter like champion show dogs.

Finn lay down, resting his chin on his front paws as he looked up, as if apologizing. Bliss was extremely comfortable with her diva status and wore it proudly.

The twins came out of the bathroom with oversized fluffy towels wrapped around them. "They love getting their hair done."

Pulling their brushes from a drawer, she combed Abilene's hair while Abilene combed Evelyn's. Abilene looked in the mirror, and tears filled her big eyes. Bliss licked her face, and Finn rested his chin on her hand.

Evelyn ran to their bedroom, then came back with scissors. "I'll cut my hair, then we'll match."

"Oh no." Savannah gently took the scissors from her. "I don't think that's a good idea."

"No!" Abilene cried out. "It's good we don't have the same hair. Then people can tell us apart. I just wish mine wasn't so—"

she tilted her head "—silly looking." Her gaze met Savannah's in the mirror. "Please cut the other side for me?"

"Oh, I don't know. I'm sure your dad wants to take you to a professional hairdresser. You have beautiful hair." There was a ribbon hanging on the wall full of clips, and the opened drawer was full of headbands and ties. "We can fix it with clips or bows."

"Please just cut it off so I'm not crooked."

"I'll do it." Sitting on the counter, Evelyn combed the long side of her sister's hair and reached for the scissors.

"No." Savannah's heart raced at the thought of one twin cutting the other's hair. Once, as a teenager, she had cut Reno's hair, thinking she was helping, and it didn't turn out so well. Her mother and sister had been furious, and poor Reno had had to shave his head—at the age of eleven. It didn't go over well at school. More evidence to prove that she should not be left alone with kids.

"I have a friend in town, Kelly Carter. She owns a salon and does remarkable things with hair. She has since we were in high school. If we need to meet her before school starts in the morning, I'm sure we can. Once we go downstairs, I'll ask your dad. If he says yes, I'll call her."

"Okay. But can you cut it just a little for now? I feel uneven."

Savannah knew that once the girls were alone Evelyn would try her best to even her sister's hair. She took the scissors from the older twin. "I'll trim it just enough, so the weight feels even. Then you'll wait until Kelly can fix it, agree?" She made sure to stare each girl in the eye. "Agree?"

They both nodded. "Agree." The pups sat on the counter and barked, as if they agreed too.

Savannah was out of her element. She never worried about her hair: wash, dry and braid was her daily routine. About twice a year, she had it cut to the middle of her shoulder blades. It was easier to keep it out of the way when it was this length.

After a few snips, she blew Abilene's hair dry and put on a headband to keep the now curly strands out of her face. Then she put Evelyn's in a long French braid.

Once everyone was happy with their hair, the twins went to their drawers and got their pajamas. Then they gave her a tour of their room. Most of the toys were downstairs, but here they had shelves full of books and their favorite dolls. The set of twin beds each had a lineup of stuffed animals. Everything looked new.

That was odd, right? She didn't know a lot about kids, but her nieces and nephew all had that favorite buddy from their toddler years that had been loved to bare threads. They had to be resewn and have pieces reattached.

Maybe Greyson had just tossed anything that was worn out or broken. It was not her business.

"Are you ready to go help put dinner together?" she said.

"Yes," the twins answered at the same time. They held hands.

"Great. Your dad is very tired tonight. So the plan is to keep everything simple and then go to bed."

Evelyn nodded and let Bliss kiss her face. "Daddy's sad because we talked about Mommy. We shouldn't have done that." She looked at her sister. "We were bad today, and that made him even more sadder."

Savannah wanted to hug them both so tightly all the melancholy would pop out. That's what her mom used to do when she was dejected. She'd hug her and tickle her until nothing was left but laughter. But she wasn't sure how to handle this.

"Today was a horrible, terrible day."

Abilene pulled Finn to her and rubbed her face in his fur.

"I was about your age when I lost my dad. My mom would get sad sometimes, then she would pretend to be happy. But she said talking about him kept him with us, and as long as we remembered him, he would be here. We all get out of sorts when we miss someone we love. But it also means we had someone to love." She laid her hand flat over her heart.

Sitting on the bed, she patted the spaces next to her. The twins sat. "It's okay to be sad, but it's also okay to have good days where you laugh and play. Are you ready to go downstairs and help your dad?"

They nodded and leaped from the bed. "I know what I'm going to pick for dinner."

"Me too." Abilene chased after her sister.

Finn stopped at the door and looked back at her. "I'm coming." Picking Finn up, she rubbed his now soft, clean fur. He licked her chin. "How did I end up in this position?" she asked him. "Of all my family members, I'm the one least equipped to help a family make a special evening from a disaster kind of day."

The part that made her question everything that she knew to be true about herself was that she could see herself in the kitchen with them. Not as their mother, but as someone that was a part of their lives. The idea of being responsible for their safety still terrified her, but the thought of hanging out and watching them grow settled deeply in her heart.

Now *she* wanted to cry. She had been perfectly happy focusing on a new life without entanglements. Why this shift?

But tonight was not about her. It was about a family who had lost their mother and the pain of being the ones left behind.

A voice drifted up the stairs. Someone new was here and talking to Greyson. Midway down, she froze. There was no way she was hearing this correctly. That sounded like her mother's voice. What was she doing here? Had Savannah been whining too much, so God thought she needed help?

She closed her eyes. *Reno*. Reno had told her mother what had happened and that she was going to help with the girls and make dinner, so of course her sweet mother, knowing that Savannah didn't have the first clue about taking care of a family, had rushed over to make everything right.

"The poor *masita* tries, but she's good at other things." She could see her mother's sweet smile as she talked to Greyson. "I have been where you are. Losing a spouse, raising children, trying to keep it all together. Take my word for it, you can't do it alone. And now you don't have to. You have the Espinozas."

"You call her *small cake*? That's what *masita* means, right?"

"*Sí*. Tiny sweet cake. Her father called her that. Her older sisters can be, um…a bit bossy and opinionated, but not Savannah. She was always a sweet girl who went along with everything."

Savannah's hand gripped the railing.

"Daddy. Did you pick your food?" Evelyn bounded into the kitchen. She stopped when she saw the visitor. Abilene bumped into her.

"Eevee!" The second twin stepped around and gasped. With wide eyes, they stared at the newcomer. "Oh. Do we have a new nanny?" She sounded disappointed.

No one had ever, not once in her life, preferred her over her mother or sisters. Savannah's heart hugged itself.

"No." Greyson's voice was clear, but a little bewildered. "This is Mrs. Espinoza, Savannah's mother. She came to help with dinner."

The girls looked from him to where Savannah was sure her mother was commanding the kitchen, stirring several pots on the stove. Savannah made her way closer but didn't go in yet.

Her mother laughed. "I have *fideo*. It's one

of Savannah's favorites. And chicken enchiladas. There is roasted squash with *papas* from my garden and beans. Of course, I brought fresh tortillas too. There should be enough for a couple of meals." She heard her mother move toward the girls. "What's wrong, *mijas*?"

"Savannah said we could have a dinner extravaganza and we'd each get to bring one thing to the table." Evelyn eyed the pantry door with longing.

"It's our mother's birthday, and we were going to help Daddy make her special brownies with ice cream."

"Oh, *sí. Sí.* Yes, your *papi* told me that. My dear Savannah is wonderful at making beautiful things with wood, but she can't cook to save her life. Have you already picked something? We can add it."

She was being ridiculous, hiding in the hallway. Taking a deep breath, she stepped into the kitchen.

"*Mami*? What are you doing here?" Savannah stood in the archway, not stepping all the way into the room.

Her mother abandoned the pot and pans she was hovering over and went to Savannah. "I came to help. Reno told me about what a special day this is." She turned to the girls.

"We are going to honor your mother. Now, you said you had something you wanted to add to Savannah's extravaganza?"

Abilene went to the refrigerator, and Evelyn dove into the pantry. Mrs. Espinoza gave Greyson a kind smile. "If you gather the things for your brownies, we can get those started so they will be ready after dinner. And the table needs to be cleared and set. It's important to sit as a family."

"Mom," Savannah said in a strained whisper, "this is not your house."

"Of course not, *tonta*. Now, go do what I told you."

"I'm not being silly. Greyson and I had this under control."

He cleared his throat. "It's okay, Savannah. I appreciate the help. You had a long day too."

Abilene plopped sliced ham with cubed cheese on the counter, and Evelyn added a bag of Cheetos. "Will these go with our dinner?"

Her mother hugged the girls. "*Perfecto*. I love your hair, by the way."

"Thank you. Daddy, do you see Abilene's hair? It looks nice, doesn't it?"

The twins held hands as they looked at him, waiting for his reaction. He knelt in front of them and cupped the side of Abilene's head. "It looks very nice. Did Savannah cut it for you?"

"Savannah." Her mother's tone took her back to being a child and getting caught making a very bad decision.

Could the ground just open and swallow her up now?

"Thank you, Savannah." His direct stare and calm voice anchored her. Then he gave his attention to the girls but spoke to Savannah's mother. "Today was a rough day for us all. There was an incident at school, and half of Abilene's hair was cut off. Savannah saved the day in more than one way even before she offered to help with dinner."

"Savannah? She has always been my most creative child. But I'm glad Reno called. When she was little and her sisters were underfoot in the kitchen wanting to know how to make things, she wanted to go out to the woodshop with her dad. Even during cartoon time, instead of watching TV, she'd be following her father around. She never learned to cook. The poor girl can't cook a frozen pizza."

Heat climbed her neck, probably turning it red. This wouldn't work. She didn't want anyone to feel sorry for her. Instead of standing here dreaming about curling up in a ball, she could put on a smile and fake her way through dinner. She had learned to do that very well.

Huge Texas beauty-queen smile in place, Savannah threw her hands high over her head and waved them. "You forget to set the timer once, and you're banned from the kitchen for life."

Her mother shook her head. "Don't over-react. It was much more than once. And she was never banned from the kitchen, just the stove." She went back to manning the pots. "It's okay. God made us all for different purposes. Savannah knows she doesn't have a domestic bone in her body, but she is very hardworking and has the kindest heart. It's good when we know our gifts and our limits. Now, who is setting the table?"

Chapter Six

Greyson wasn't sure what to do with the small woman who had taken over his kitchen. She was unloading foil-wrapped containers from bags, turning on his oven and talking a mile a minute. Some of it might have been in Spanish. She seemed to be talking to herself half the time. And now she'd made it sound as though Savannah didn't like children, cooking or anything else domestic.

It was easy to see that Savannah didn't fall into any feminine stereotypes, but she was great with the girls. Better than anyone had been since they'd lost their mother. Her family didn't understand her.

He knew how that felt. Jessica's family had been very opinionated about where they should live and what they should be doing. They'd never really approved of him. Maybe they were right. In the end he hadn't been able to protect her.

But tonight he wanted to focus on the girls and try to salvage the last bit of this day. He had the twins gather the supplies to make the brownies.

They laughed as they helped beat the batter. He glanced over at Savannah to check on her. She stood at his dining room table.

The table was still covered with taped-up boxes.

The items in those boxes were connected to memories. The tangible connections to their past that he was supposed to wipe clean.

Stop.

He rubbed his head and focused on the girls. They deserved to make new memories, even if they were built on lies, and it hurt that Jessica wouldn't be a part of them.

That thought slammed into his heart. Had that been what he was doing? Feeling guilty about making new memories with them because their mother wouldn't be a part of them? This epiphany hit him hard and needed to be processed, but there was no time.

Savannah opened a box and looked inside it, then closed it and scanned the room. She looked as lost as he felt. He had the twins take turns with the spoon.

"Hey, Savannah," Greyson called out to her.

"Yeah?"

"Could you do me a favor?"

Her expression opened with hope and eagerness. He was a little irritated at Mrs. Espinoza. He knew she was just trying to help, but he missed the spontaneous joy Savannah had brought to his home earlier.

"Sure. What is it?"

"The boxes on the far end of the table have plates and glasses. Tonight calls for more than plastic and paper. Would you mind getting them out? You can throw the empty boxes in the office."

Going to the other end of the table she opened the first box and pulled out a pretty blue plate with tiny hand-painted flowers in a darker blue. Jessica had found those plates on a trip to Mexico, and her sister had bought the whole set for their wedding.

"Greyson." Mrs. Espinoza's gentle voice pulled his attention away from the dark edge of his thoughts. Tonight, with the help of Savannah and her mom, they would open the boxes. Most were the new items he had never seen. He mixed those in with a few old ones. It was good to make new memories with them. It needed to be done.

"Yes, ma'am."

"I just want you to know how grateful I am for you letting Savannah into your daughters' lives. It's good for her to be around kids. She has her reasons, but she has avoided getting close to children. *Gracias*."

He glanced at Savannah. Could she hear her mother? Her posture was a little stiff as she moved to the next box.

"Mrs. Espinoza, I'm the one grateful for Savannah. You've raised an incredible daughter. She's been here for my girls since day one. She's a natural with them. If she weren't so good at restoring my barns, I'd offer her any price to be my nanny."

Savannah froze. When she looked up, their eyes met. *Oh no.* She looked like she was going to cry. How was he making this worse?

Not sure what to do, he helped the twins pour the batter into the baking pan and slid it into the oven. His girls ran straight to Savannah. Arms crossed, he watched as she went down to their level. How could her mother be so wrong about her?

"Savannah, we put the brownies in the oven. Daddy said to come to help you. Are there candlesticks?" Evelyn climbed on a chair. She lifted a vase from a box with a national furniture-store logo. "Oh, this is pretty. We have to have flowers."

Someone from the federal government purchased everything he would need to set up a new home. No link to the past. No echoes of Jessica's love of color and uniqueness.

Abilene tilted her head. "I can get the paper flowers we made."

Savannah nodded. "That's a good idea. A picture would be nice too. We can put it on the table. I think I saw candles in this box."

Abilene ran to their playroom, and Evelyn opened the next box. Soon they had plates, glasses, silverware and the candlesticks set up around the table. He wasn't sure which unsettled him more: the generic mass-produced pieces or the few dishes he had managed to keep.

His fingers traced the organic edge of a colorful plate. Memories rushed him, and he stepped away for a minute. That was all he needed, just enough time not to drown. He wanted the memories, cherished them, but the first wave was hard.

There would be no new memories with her. His throat burned, but he would not let the girls see him upset, not right now. The day had just become their mother's birthday instead of the day she was taken from them. He closed his eyes. So many lies.

He needed to get Savannah and her mother

out as quickly as possible. The less people he was forced to lie to, the better.

Abilene returned and handed a bouquet of paper flowers to her sister. "I also brought a picture of Mommy." She tried to whisper so that only Savannah and Evelyn would hear her.

He had to smile. Jessica had never been able to master the art of whispering either. *Wait*. A picture. Where had she gotten a picture?

"Do you think it will upset Daddy if I put it on the table?"

They weren't supposed to have any pictures of their past life. That had been a hard rule.

"You have a picture of your mom?" He tried to sound casual.

Her eyes were wide, as if she'd gotten caught stealing cookies. Abilene turned to her father. "I'm sorry, Daddy. I made one. Just for the house. Can we put a picture of Mommy on the table, just for tonight? So when we sing Happy Birthday, we can sing to her?"

She had drawn a picture of the mother she probably didn't have any clear memories of despite the face on this one. His heart burned, the pressure in his chest so tight he had to take a moment to breathe before he could respond.

"Of course." He knelt in front of Abilene. How long had they been protecting his feelings? "It's pretty. Just like her."

His daughter nodded. "I used purple, her favorite color."

The picture had a figure in a purple dress with long curly red hair. His girls didn't have a real recollection of their mother's appearance. A surge of anger burned from his core. They deserved to at least know what their mother looked like, to see her holding them, laughing with them. In every picture, love had lit Jessica's face.

Taking a deep breath to get his emotions under control, he looked up and found Savannah staring at him. She bit her lip and turned away.

Great. She had to think this was all weird. He wanted to explain to her why this was unsettling, why they didn't have a single picture of his wife, their mother. Or of the girls growing up.

For the first time since he'd lost Jessica, he wanted to reach out and touch another woman's hand and share his frustrations and doubts.

Gritting his teeth, he pushed all that messiness aside. As long as the girls were young and that man could be a threat, he would have to do this alone. No relationships, no…love.

"Daddy, is it okay that I drew this picture?"

"It's a beautiful picture," Savannah said, as she knelt in front of his daughter. She shifted her gaze to him and raised her brows.

He cleared the thickness from his throat. "Yes, Abilene, the picture is a good idea. Thank you for thinking of it. It reminds me of the time your mother took you to the park to have your first ice cream cone." The girls came closer to him, eager for any story about the mother they lost. He couldn't let the man that killed Jessica wipe her from her girls' lives completely. "You weren't two yet, and you made such a mess. I think more of the strawberry ice cream ended up on your face and clothes than in your tummies."

They giggled, and he reached out to hug them close.

"Dinner's ready!" Savannah's mother announced, as she brought a tortilla warmer to the table.

The girls cheered and then hurried to the table.

Mrs. Espinoza went back to the kitchen, giving orders to move pots and platters to the table. Together with the girls, Savannah and

Greyson quickly brought in the food. "Daddy, we need to light the candles."

With everything in place, including the twins, he lit the tall, tapered candles, then sat down at the head of the table.

"This is very nice. What a wonderful way to celebrate your mother's life." Mrs. Espinoza turned to him. "Will you lead us in a prayer of thanksgiving?" she asked.

With a nod, they all joined hands, and he lifted his little family up to God. In the middle of the prayer, he had to stop. His chest became so tight that no words could form.

This was what the girls were missing. When was the last time they saw his faith in action? Seated on either side of him, the girls squeezed his hands.

Evelyn picked up the prayer. "Thank You for giving us our Mommy, and please make sure she knows we wish her a happy birthday. She is with You now, so I know she is happy. Thank You for Daddy, and please help all his flowers grow. Thank You for Savannah. And please forgive me for getting mad at Caty. Even though she did hurt my sister. That's all I have for now. Amen."

Keeping his head down a little longer, he blinked back the tears and hid his grin. He returned the gentle pressure to the twins' hands, then let go of them.

"Thank you for finishing the prayer for me."

Evelyn nodded. "You're welcome. It's okay not to be able to talk. It happens to me sometimes too. Your heart mashes so tight you just can't do anything but sit there quiet as a mouse."

He leaned over and kissed the top of her head. Then, not wanting to cry, he grabbed the bowl closest to him and served his daughters. "There's lots of food here, so dig in. Your mother would have loved everything here."

"Since this is all about your mother," Savannah said, passing the tortilla warmer to Abilene, "who wants to share a memory?"

The girls stared at each other, then looked to him. There was an awkward silence.

Evelyn spoke first. "I remember songs. Did she like to sing, Daddy?"

"She did. Every morning she would greet you with a song and sing you to sleep at night. She sang all day. Sometimes she would just sing her words." He smiled at the memory. Surely there was nothing dangerous in telling them this story of their mother.

Abilene sat up. "I remember. You are my sunshine…"

Evelyn nodded and joined her. They ended with the last line their mother had made up "… I love you forever and a day."

Greyson grinned. "I told your mother she got the song wrong, but she claimed to have changed it because it was her song to you."

Joy radiated from Abilene in a way it hadn't since the last time she was with her mom. "I can hear her voice, Daddy." Eyes closed, she sang. "You are so beautiful." The words low and raspy. The way Jessica had sung it to the girls every day. It was the song she sang the first time they were put in her arms.

As the children repeated the lyrics, a flood of nostalgia swept over him, threatening to pull him under. Yolanda, Savannah's mother, smiled. He changed the topic and told stories about Finn and Bliss. It worked. The girls talked about their puppies and their favorite things at school.

He was asked about the farm. Conversation was smooth and easy. The girls were more animated. Setting the table, having guests— it all seemed so normal.

He had missed this. His girls did, too, even if they didn't understand how to explain the void.

He wanted this for them. Leaning back, meal forgotten, he watched Savannah. She was telling them a story about the first time she went riding. She was so much more than he'd expected. She was bonding with his daughters, and they were absorbing all this female attention.

During the trial he had been hyper focused on his daughters' safety. The man had not only taken Jessica, but the girls' childhood too.

Maybe there was a way Savannah could help with that, but in what capacity? There could never be anything between them, not with all the lies he had to live with now. But there had to be a way to give Evelyn and Abilene more of this.

He shook his head and went back to his meal. It was selfish asking anything more from her. Especially since he had nothing to give her in return.

Savannah loved hearing the girls' happy chatter. Greyson even looked more at ease. As much as her mother could push her to the edge, she adored and admired her. That amazing woman had always been able to work wonders on short notice. She would never be anything close to the woman her mother was.

Looking at the artsy plates mixed in with

the new table settings, she could tell that Greyson's wife had been the kind of woman her mother would admire. Why were there only a few of the unique dishes and so many brand-new items? She was pretty sure they had just unboxed them for the first time since his arrival.

What was going on?

She glanced at the drawing Abilene had made. Her stomach twisted, chasing off any appetite she had built up since lunch. Not a single picture of their mother. He had jumped at her to not take a picture earlier.

Something was wrong.

"Savannah," Evelyn called to her, "thank you for bringing your mom. This is the best dinner. Our mom would have loved this. Right, Daddy?"

"She would have."

Her mother laughed. "Oh, it's nothing special. A little extra creamy cheese and love. Tell me what your favorite meal was your mother made for you."

The girls looked at Greyson. Once again it seemed as if they were asking permission to talk about their mother, or they had no memories of her.

"She…she loved baking. And she was always trying out new meals." He pushed the beans into the rice. "Savannah says she is one of seven. I can't keep up with two. Any words of wisdom?"

"We do what we must for our children. My older girls were so helpful. I don't know how I would have made it without them." She smiled at her daughter. "Savannah was her father's shadow. All she wanted to do was be outside. His death probably left her the most lost."

Stabbing a piece of cheesy enchilada and running it through her refried beans, she tried to swallow another bite. It stopped midway to her mouth, and she let it drop to the pretty plate. Without tasting it, she knew it would be effortlessly perfect, just like her mother and sisters.

Her mother was now telling the girls how Margarita and Josefina had always made cards and special desserts to make everyone feel better, and now they had their own shop.

Dropping the fork in defeat, she shook the melancholy out of her head. It would upset her mother if she had any clue this conversation was hurting her. To her family, it was just a simple fact. Savannah was different.

Domestic skills came easily for the Espinoza family. Everyone knew it was embedded in their DNA. DNA Savannah didn't get.

A gentle hand covered her wrist. "*Mija, que?* Is being here for this long too much?" Her mother glanced at the girls. "I know being around kids is not your favorite thing, but you have done God's work tonight. You gave them what they needed."

She made sure to give her mother a smile. "It's not that, Mom. I really have enjoyed being here for them." There was no way she could even begin to explain how she thought Greyson was hiding something.

She knew she wouldn't. Confrontation that could hurt someone left her a little ill. And there was no way she would ever confess to her family that they had hurt her feelings, especially her mom.

It would devastate her mother if she learned that anything she said or did made Savannah feel unworthy.

Then, for the next hour, she would reassure Savannah that she was as she was because that was how God had made her. And that would only make her feel worse. Her mother had sacrificed so much for them. Savannah never wanted to be the cause of pain for her mother.

The timer went off, causing the twins to jump from their chairs and run to the oven. "Are the brownies ready?" They hunched over and peered in the small window. Savannah's mother pulled it out and showed the twins how to check to see if it was done. "It must cool. Would you like to make your mom a special card while we wait?"

"Yes!"

"Can we have two scoops of ice cream when it's ready?" Evelyn asked.

"One scoop is enough," Greyson said, in a very fatherly-sounding voice.

"Go make your cards. That should give us time to let the brownies cool. Then it's time for bed."

"Daddy—"

"Nope. In the morning, we have to take care of the mess at school." He gave a side-eye to his youngest with her uneven curls as they ran to the playroom.

"You must come over for Sunday dinner. You can meet all my children," Mrs. Espinoza announced.

"Do any of your children cut hair?" Greyson asked.

"I have a friend that does," Savannah said. "I can text her tonight to see if she can cut Evelyn's hair in the morning before school."

"You don't mind?"

"No. Consider it done." She took her phone out and sent the text.

"Greyson." Her mother was moving dishes to the sink. "We really should make a play-date with your girls and my grandchildren. You and Josefina have so much in common, and being single parents, you could help each other out. And there is Resa. She is a midwife and is so good with children."

Savannah couldn't believe it. Her mother was setting up Greyson with her sisters. She rolled her eyes. Of course, as an incurable romantic she loved playing matchmaker. And her mother was probably right, as usual. Josefina and Greyson would make a good couple, and her niece would love the twins.

"Um, I uh…" Greyson stalled under the twist in the conversation. "We're really busy with getting everything ready for the first harvest. I don't know—"

"Mom, everyone in town has been trying to set him up. As great as Josefina is, he's not interested." There, she said it. He could thank her later.

Her mother raised an eyebrow at Savannah's assertive tone. Greyson was turning red. Had she overstepped?

"I'm sorry," she said quickly. "My mother means well, but she has been known to steamroll people into doing what she thinks is best."

"*Mija*," her mother said in her most offended voice, "that is not true. He's new in town. Everyone needs friends and connections." She turned to Greyson. "Josefina is the PTO president. She knows everyone and can help navigate any problems that come up at school."

"That is true," Savannah told Greyson.

Her mother smiled at Greyson and patted his hand. "Sorry if I said the wrong thing, but still you should come for Sunday dinner after church. We have an open door. You already know Reno and Savannah. You should meet everyone else."

Greyson gave her a polite smile.

Savannah's phone pinged. "It's Kelly. She says she can do the cut if we can get there an hour and a half before school starts. Does that work?" She looked up and found herself alone with Greyson. Her mother had gone into the kitchen.

"Thank you," he said.

"It's no problem. If you want, we can start the day with a special treat at my sisters' bakery. But be warned—once the twins taste the sweets my sisters create, they will be begging to go every morning."

She reached for a bowl to take into the kitchen, but his hand covered her wrist and stopped her. Brows raised, she looked up at him.

He just stared at her for a moment. Then he shook his head, confusion wrinkling the space between his brows. "Not just for the hair appointment. I don't get it. Your mom goes on about how awkward you are with kids and that you don't have a domestic instinct in your entire body." He shook his head. "That doesn't make sense. You're great with my girls, and they've become very prickly with strangers since…in the last few years. What gives?"

Heat climbed up her neck. This was so embarrassing. "My connection to your girls is a fluke. Ask anyone in town. I'll do anything not to be alone with kids, and no one wants me to be alone with them, anyway. So it works out."

"It's not a fluke. Savannah, look at me." He waited for her to lower her gaze to his. "You're amazing with the twins. I wouldn't trust anyone else with them right now."

Everything inside her went soft, and she swallowed down the irrationally emotional responses to this simple praise. He didn't realize what he was saying, that was all. She forced a laugh. "Goes to show what happens when you're new in town and don't know what to watch out for."

"No. It's more like this small town has labeled you for some reason. How can your family not see you?"

A loud sound that might have been laughter erupted from her. Much louder than she intended. She glanced across the kitchen into the playroom. Yeah, they were all looking now. She could see the question in her mother's face from across the two rooms that separated them. Why was she so awkward? "Sorry."

He opened his mouth to reply, but her mother guided the twins into the kitchen. "The cards are made, and the brownies are *perfecto* for serving with the ice cream. Are we ready?"

"Yes!" the girls agreed as one.

"Savannah." He stopped her from moving forward. "I really need to talk to you. I know it's been a long day, but can you stay a bit after I get the girls to bed? I have something important to ask you."

Not having a clue what to say, she nodded.

"Great. Come on, let's get some ice cream."

Her mind whirled. What did he need to ask her that he couldn't address now?

"It's time for me to go," her mother suddenly announced.

"No," the girls said around mouths full of dessert.

She kissed them on the forehead and headed to the door. On her way out, she put her arm through Savannah's. Still bewildered by Greyson, she went along without a word.

At the front door, her mother turned to her. "I'm sorry I didn't see it earlier, *masita*. I promise no more setting him up. I'll let everyone else know he is yours."

"What? No. Mom!" She looked over her shoulder and, even though they were out of sight and earshot of the kitchen, she lowered her voice. "He is *not* mine. I have no idea what you are talking about."

With a twinkle in her eye and an all-knowing smirk, her mother patted her cheek. "God knows best. So much more than I do. I would have never put the two of you together. I'm sure that's the reason I was so slow on seeing the truth. But it's okay. We are all here to help you, however you need it. This will be a challenge for you, but you have to go for it."

"Mother," she said through clenched teeth. "There is nothing to go for. It's not like that."

Her mother laughed. "Okay. Whatever you say. But I know what I know. And it will be all good. I'll leave the back-door light on for you. Don't be too late." Without giving Savannah another chance to explain, she walked out the door.

Savannah rubbed her temple. By the time her mother pulled into their driveway, she would have already talked to all her siblings. They were all going to think…going to think that she liked Greyson. *Like*-liked him. This was so humiliating. There was no way she could walk into that bakery in the morning.

Now she had to go back into the kitchen and wait for whatever question he was going to ask her. It would only be fair to warn him that the Espinoza group chat had been activated and that he was the subject.

With a deep breath, she headed back to the kitchen.

Her mother wasn't completely wrong. How did she pick up on feelings Savannah was trying to hide from herself? She sighed.

Her brain and heart were playing volleyball with mixed emotions. What her mother didn't know was that Greyson was not looking for any sort of relationship. There wasn't room in his life for another romance. Not that she would ever fit that role, anyway.

And the more time she spent with Greyson and the girls, the more questions she had. The girls loved their father, but it was becoming increasingly obvious that there was something going on.

Had God put her here to help the girls?

Other than restoring the barns, she wasn't sure what she had to offer this little family. Maybe she was here so that Greyson and his daughters would meet her family. She was the connector. He should be with someone like Josefina. They would be a nice match. She was okay with that.

She was.

Greyson paused as he put the unpacked dishes in the cabinet. Now that it was done, it was good to see the little bit of Jessica in the new house. He could convince Savannah to help with the other boxes. She would be focused on the job without getting buried in memories or resenting the new items that had nothing to do with Jessica. He had wasted enough time and energy on regrets. It wouldn't help the twins.

He also needed Savannah's help with the girls, but he wasn't sure how to make it work without taking advantage of her kindness.

Her mother had been amazing, but he didn't understand how she thought Savannah wouldn't be good around the kids. Was he missing something?

"Daddy, we washed our hands. Can we watch a movie with Bliss and Finn?"

"For thirty minutes."

Savannah came back into the kitchen and, without saying a word, put the leftovers in the refrigerator. Closing the door, she leaned against it. "I'm so sorry about my mother. She is amazing and wonderful in so many ways, but she is not subtle, and she believes she knows best. Be warned. As we speak, she is telling the family that we are…" She turned from him.

"We are…?"

"I'm not sure. She's playing matchmaker, so I'm sure she's somehow convincing everyone we're dating." She dropped her gaze, then took a deep breath and lifted it to meet his. "I'm so sorry. I'll try my best to convince them she's way off the mark."

"I got the impression she was trying to set me up with your sister. Thank you, by the way, for having my back on that one."

"Yeah. Well, I might have done too good a job. She thinks I've claimed you."

"Claimed me. Like a lost-and-found item?" He laughed. "That might work out for me."

Her eyes couldn't have gone any wider. "What? I don't think you understood what I just said. My mom is going to be telling everyone that we are dating. Like we—" she waved a hand between them "—are a couple."

Leaning one hip against the counter, he

crossed his arms over his chest. "Sounds like your mom might be onto something. It would put a stop to everyone in town trying to bring me casseroles and set me up with their granddaughter or cousin." This would solve so many of his problems. He grinned, feeling an unfamiliar sting of hope.

"This is not funny. It's a disaster."

"Daddy, my tummy hurts." Abilene came into the kitchen before he could reply to Savannah's doomsday attitude. His daughter laid her head against him, and he went down on his haunches.

"How about we get you settled into bed and I read your favorite story?"

"It's way past time for me to go." Savannah was backing out of the kitchen.

He stood, not ready for her to leave. "Join us for dinner tomorrow, and we'll talk some more about your mom's idea."

She tilted her head as if she didn't understand what he'd said, then shook her head. "No. I have plans tomorrow after work, but I'll be here first thing in the morning to help with the girls. You can head to the school and get all that straightened out while I take them to Kelly."

"Daddy, I don't want to go to school."

Abilene hugged him tighter. "My tummy really hurts."

He kissed her forehead. "It's going to be okay." He looked at Savannah. She had one eye on the door. There wouldn't be any more conversation about his plan tonight, but she'd be back in the morning. Having a pretend girlfriend who helped with the girls would solve so many problems.

And with most of his life being made-up, it seemed ironically appropriate.

He would just have to be patient. Not his strongest character trait.

Chapter Seven

Soft light preceded the sun rising. It gently caressed the farm, highlighting the trees and roofs. Her breath fogged the air in front of her. Late last night, the temperature had dropped drastically. Winter had returned.

Savannah knocked on the door and stepped back, her head lowered. She was mentally steeling herself to see Greyson. She was just here to help the girls. Little girls who didn't have a single picture of their mother. Unease nibbled at the edge of her stomach.

Greyson seemed just as lost...or else it was all an act. Getting weird about Greyson would make things awkward, and it didn't have to be. *Don't make this awkward, says Miss Queen of Awkward to herself.*

Deep breath. Be normal. She tapped on the door again.

Not being from a small town, Greyson just didn't understand the damage her mother was doing. He thought it was a joke. *Whatever.*

She was going to ignore these feelings and be normal. If she didn't get involved with him, then it didn't matter what he was lying about. None of her business.

But when it came to her mother and the plans she made for her family, ignoring her was not a solid option, right? Going along with it would only invite trouble, and she'd had enough of that. She and God had made a deal: she would not be led astray, and He would help her find her spark.

The twins opened the door, smiles on their faces for her. She sighed with relief and gave them a hug. She didn't have to pretend to be happy to see them. "Good morning, beautifuls."

The girls smiled back. "Good morning, Savannah." They were dressed and ready to go.

Evelyn reached for her hand. Grabbing it, she pulled Savannah into the house. "I told Daddy I want to get my hair cut too. But he said no. Can you tell him I should? It'll make Abilene feel better if we both get it done."

"Oh." Telling Greyson what he should do with his daughters didn't sound like a good idea. "Uh... I—"

"Evelyn Rebecca McKinsey." They all jumped at his voice. "Are you trying to convince Savannah to change my mind about you?" Greyson was wearing another buttoned-up dress shirt with his hair combed back. He didn't look like a farmer. Which was good, because Farmer Greyson was a lot easier to like. He was more comfortable to be around. Businessman Greyson was sleek eye candy, but so intimidating and aloof. Oh no. It was bad. This man intrigued her. But he shouldn't. He was hiding something. Was it big or small? Either way she was in trouble.

In front of him, stuff to make sandwiches was laid out on the kitchen counter. He was packing their lunches. Why did that make her heart melt a little? Millions of parents packed lunches every morning.

He put his hands on his hips and tilted his head as he gave his daughter a narrow-eyed stare. "This is an impulse decision. Just because Abilene has to cut hers doesn't mean you need yours cut."

"I've thought about it all night, Daddy. You said we're starting over in an all-new life. So we can also have new haircuts. It'll be strange if Abilene gets one and I don't. I don't want people to laugh at her."

His features softened. "No one is going to

laugh at her—and if they do, how will cutting off your hair help? Just because your sister is getting something doesn't mean you have to. You're individuals."

Savannah remembered when she was their age and being so hurt and confused about the loss of her father. She had wanted a pair of boots like his, but everyone had told her no.

She put her arm around Evelyn. "Change can be good." She glanced over at Abilene, who'd been quiet. "Sometimes we don't get to pick the change, but other times we do. Do you really want to change your hair?" She stayed focused on the girls, kneeling in front of them. The need to comfort them was stronger than the worry about Greyson lying or being upset at her interference.

Evelyn laid her head against Savannah and was silent for a moment. Then she nodded and turned to her father. "Please, Daddy. I do want to cut my hair too."

He sighed, picked up the lunches and came around to hand the bags to the girls. "Okay, I'll leave it up to you. It's your hair." He held up a finger, then bumped his daughter's nose. "But no colors."

The girls giggled. Savannah gave a huge gasp. "Not even purple and pink with glitter?"

"Daddy, I want purple with glitter." Evelyn fluttered her eyelashes in fake innocence. Full-out laughter filled the kitchen.

He shook his head, but the grin looked good on him. "No, not until you're at least twenty. Make that thirty. When you're living on your own."

"But we're going to always live with you, Daddy."

"We'll see how you feel about that when you're twenty." Walking to the dining room, he reached for a gray suit jacket and slipped it on. Of course, it fitted perfectly to his broad shoulders. The businessman was full-on again.

She looked away. "The Texas weather is having a mood swing. It's cold out this morning, so I recommend coats. If you want to go ahead to the school, I can take the girls to Kelly for the haircuts." She tried again to not get in the same car as him.

Greyson crossed his arms and stared at her the same way he'd been staring at his daughters earlier. "We'll all go in my car. No reason to take two vehicles back into town. I'll drop you off at the hair salon and go to the school. When I'm finished, we can go to the bakery. We haven't been yet. Then it's to school for them, and we'll have time to talk before we get the day started on the farm."

Her stomach tightened at the thought of them going to the bakery together. Her sisters would have so much to say about that. Then they would be driving back to the farm in the car alone. So they could talk. Dread tightened her stomach.

There went her plan to lie low from her family, while also avoiding him. She had already picked the twins up from school. Now they were going to be seen in town at the hair salon and then at her sisters' bakery. This was not going to help.

Maybe she could use this time to explain to him how small-town gossip worked. Her mother was the best at derailing gossip and putting a stop to it, but with her leading the charge today, there would be no hope of slowing the spread.

"Come on, let's go!" He headed down the hallway, picking up his keys on the way to the door. The girls got coats out of the hallway closet and ran straight to his car. He waited for her.

"Savannah, what's wrong?"

The list was too long. She shook her head. Why was she so drawn to him when he was obviously not being honest about his past?

She had a problem. She had to get over herself. "Nothing. I'm fine." She headed out the door.

He touched her arm as he closed the door behind them. "*Nothing. I'm fine*?" He repeated her words in a flat voice. "That is usually code for *My problems are so bad that I can't fix them, so the only thing left to do is give up.* What's wrong?"

Why couldn't he be like everyone else and just accept that she was fine? He held her arm and stared at her, waiting.

She looked at him, then to the sky. Each minute, more rays of light came over the eastern horizon. "You and me, being seen in town together. This is just going to stir up the gossip even faster. Maybe we shouldn't go to the bakery."

"I already told the twins we're going. No takebacks." He laughed. "And the town's already gossiping about me. Every time I go in, someone is trying to fix me up. Some of the ladies are so bold as to actually drive out here. If they think I'm *claimed*," he hooked his fingers in air quotes, "I'll be less interesting. It makes life easier."

They stood at the passenger door, his fingers on the handle. She studied his face. "There is nothing easy about this."

"I have a plan, of sorts. Please, hear me out. It can help both of us. Well, I know selfishly it'll help me the most. But we'll talk about the details once the girls get dropped off at school." He opened the door and waited for her to get in.

Oh no. That did not sound good. *He had a plan.* When people in her life had plans, things never went well for her.

The girls were in the back seat, buckled up. She got in and put on her seat belt, then stared straight ahead. Her mother and sisters were going to love this at first. Then it would all become drama when they realized that she didn't really mean anything to him.

"I want to get a pixie cut," Abilene said.

"Pixie cut? How do you even know what that is?" Greyson asked her.

Her eyes went wide, and she looked at her sister. Uh-oh, they'd done something they weren't supposed to do. Savannah bit back a grin. They looked *so* guilty.

Greyson glanced up into the rearview mirror, his jaw set. "Girls, what did you do?"

Evelyn sighed as if the weight of the world sat on her shoulders. "We had to do research, Daddy. Like you did to find the best flowers for the farm. We couldn't sleep. So we went downstairs to your office and opened the laptop and typed in *short haircuts that are cute*."

He stopped the car as they were about to turn off the farm and onto the main road to town. With slow, intentional movements, he twisted around and looked each of his daughters in the eye. "How did you know the password to get into my computer?"

Evelyn shrugged. "I've seen you, Daddy."

He tilted his head back and looked at the roof of the vehicle, then closed his eyes. With a sigh, he opened them and turned to them again. "If you needed to look up hairstyles so badly, you should have woken me up. You don't ever go on the computer without me. Do you understand? Not ever. It's dangerous."

Their eyes widened under his quiet anger. They nodded.

"And my password will be changing as soon as we get home."

"You looked up haircuts?" she asked. "That was a clever idea, but you should have done that with me or your dad. We can also do that with Kelly. She has tons of magazines."

Greyson sagged back into his seat. With his hands back on the steering wheel, he moved the car toward town. His hands were shaking, and he looked so tense. She wanted to reach out and reassure him that it was okay, but she locked her fingers together in her lap.

"Daddy, I'm sorry." Abilene had her arms crossed tightly over her chest. "We couldn't sleep."

"It was all my idea," Evelyn offered herself up. "I knew your password. I didn't know how else to make Abilene feel better."

"Girls, from this minute going forward, you promise me that if you can't sleep because you're worried about something, you *will* wake me up. You have to stay off the internet." He closed his eyes. "It's not always a safe place to be. Even though you're in our house, you're going out into the world without me, and that scares me. A lot. Promise me that you won't do that again."

"We promise, Daddy." The girls were holding hands as they nodded in unison. The car fell into a heavy silence.

Savannah stared out the window as they drove past the dunes that hid the gulf. It was strange knowing that the huge, endless ocean was right there, but that it was hidden by one small bump of sand. Life was like that. Problems or solutions were just a step away, but you never saw them until you climbed the hill.

Where was she in her life? Was she close to seeing the beautiful horizon?

Abilene kept touching her hair, and Evelyn wouldn't let go of her sister's other hand. Greyson's jaw was popping, and the tension was heavy. Each had their own worries, and she didn't have a clue how to help.

Since it was the middle of the week, the main strip was empty. They drove past the bakery her two older sisters owned. She hoped they ran out of time to go there. Greyson had no clue about the minefield that innocent-looking bakery hid.

She glanced around the car. She needed something to get a smile on everyone's face, or her sisters would go into overdrive trying to identify the problem and fix it. Protectiveness over her little family flooded her system.

She gasped. No. This was not *her* family. Her family were the ones in the bakery.

"What's wrong?" Greyson glanced at her.

"Nothing. I, um… It's nothing." She cleared her throat. "I remembered something I told Reno I would do. But it's not an emergency." She bit down on her lips to stop any more words from spilling out. "It's okay."

But it wasn't. She shook her head to clear any bizarre, misplaced thoughts. Greyson and his daughters were not hers. She was just helping.

She turned to the twins with the biggest smile she could manage. Kelly's car was the only one in front of the Cutting Edge salon. Greyson dropped them off, then left for the meeting at school. She sent a prayer that it would all be worked out.

Kelly took her time cutting and styling both the girls' hair. Greyson was also gone longer than Savannah had thought he would be. Checking the time, she was relieved to see they would have to go straight to school and skip the visit to the bakery. She wasn't in the mood to deal with her sisters' meddling.

When their dad finally came in the door, the twins were excited about their new styles.

Abilene had long bangs that swept to the side with the sides fading above her ears. It made her eyes look huge. Evelyn swung her head back and forth. The longer bob cut framed her face, ending right above her shoulders.

They glowed under his attention, so Savannah hung back. They might hesitate to speak about their mom, but they obviously loved him as much as he loved them. It made her miss her father, but it also made her grateful for having had him for the time she did.

Greyson looked up.

She smiled. "They look great, don't they? They're ready for school. No more bellyaches, and no time for a stop at the bakery. Too bad."

The girls protested, but Greyson agreed with her. Savannah tried not to show her relief. "How did the meeting go?" she asked as they made their way to his SUV.

"Good news. Your classmates came forward and told them what you told me. They said that Caty had been picking on the twins since we moved here. Why didn't you tell me what was going on, girls?"

In the back seat, the twins looked at each other. Holding her sister's hand, Evelyn spoke up. "We didn't want to cause any trouble, just like you told us."

He sighed. "I know this is hard. I've told you over and over not to say things, but you have to talk to me. Together we will figure out what is important to address and what we should ignore. You can't ignore a bully." His jaw flexed.

She turned to the girls. "You need to tell her you expect to be treated with politeness, the same as you'll treat her. You don't have to be friends with her or even talk to her, but it's a small school. In the years to come, you'll always be seeing her and probably have her in a lot of your classes."

"Okay." The girls nodded as Greyson pulled up into the drop-off area. It was a little after classes started, so the lane was clear.

"I'll take them in. Do you want to come with us?"

"No." That came out a little harsher than she'd intended so she smiled. "I'll wait here." There was no way she was going to walk into that building with Greyson and his daughters as if they were some sort of family. The flicker of gossip that fluttered around them now would turn into a wildfire.

The girls had their haircuts. Good deeds had been done. Now she would return to the farm and get back to her real work. That was the job she had been hired to do.

Slipping into the car, Greyson secured his seat belt, then sat there for a moment, settling his thoughts.

"Greyson?" Concern tinged her voice. "Are the girls good?"

He nodded and started the car. "Yeah. Ms. Nichols was very welcoming. She said she'd talked to you last night and apologized for not being aware of the girls' loss." He hated that people were talking about them, but the guilt he felt over not being the one to make sure his daughters were okay was worse.

He should have been more proactive. But he was used to hiding everything. How did he balance the lies with the girls' well-being? It would be easier to homeschool, but they loved school.

Moving to a small town was supposed to make things easier, but it had brought complications he hadn't dreamed of. Now there was Savannah. He had to fight the urge to open up to her, to tell her everything. But he couldn't risk it. The girls needed her, but he was going to keep his distance.

"I'm sorry. Did I overstep? We went to school together. She's a great teacher. I thought if she knew the—"

"It's okay. That helped them a lot. I'm a very private person and I just… I don't like people knowing our business." And he should have been the one to call the teacher. Turning to Savannah, he made sure to give her a reassuring smile before focusing on the road ahead. "You've helped in more ways than I can count or properly express appreciation for."

"I didn't really do anything." She crossed her arms and leaned into the corner as she looked out the window.

Her body language screamed *Don't talk to me*. He frowned. Had he upset her? Probably. "Savannah, what's wrong? Did someone say something to you when we were inside the school?"

"No. I just want to get back to work. There's a lot to do in the barns, and Reno has already been out there a couple of hours working alone. I'm tired. All this with the girls is just not normal for me."

"I know. Like I said, I can't thank you enough. You've gone way beyond the call of duty. That's one of the reasons I wanted you to come with me this morning, so that we could have a chance to talk."

He didn't think it was possible, but she pulled tighter into herself. She looked so tense with her forehead pressed against the window. "I know you weren't happy with your mother talking about us dating, but I thought about it. Neither one of us want to date, but it seems the favorite pastimes in Port Del Mar are gossiping and matchmaking. If we let people think we're seeing each other, it solves a lot of problems. And it will seem natural for you to pick up the girls in an emergency."

She shook her head. "You want me to lie to

make your life easier. I can't do it." Her voice had a bitter edge to it.

"No. That's not what..." He was messing this up. Running a hand through his hair, he glanced at her. "I guess, in a way, it's a lie to make my life run smoother. But if you help with the girls, join us for a few meals, they would love it, and people will just assume whatever they want. We'll be clear to the twins that you're just helping so that they don't get confused. I'll pay for your time. You said you were saving up to get back to your art."

He took a short breath and plowed ahead. "Most importantly, it helps the girls. No lies." He already had too many. He sighed. "Would you at least be willing to help with them? Finding a nanny seems impossible. Nothing full-time, just pick them up occasionally if I have a late meeting. I don't know anyone in town. I trust you, and you're already on the farm. You know I'm not interested in a romantic relationship, so we don't have to worry about hurt feelings. It would be the easiest solution."

Not interested? He snorted. What's one more lie at this point? But this one was for her protection. He couldn't destroy another woman's life. It was going to take everything he had to keep his children safe. That was his only purpose in life.

She didn't say a word. He had said too much. How to get this back on track? "Savannah—"

"Listen, I'm not the most responsible to be left alone with kids. And I've proven it with yours. A couple of hours and I had them covered in mud. On a school night when they should have been doing homework. You really should talk to Josefina."

He laughed. "You do realize that when that happened, you weren't alone with them? Reno was there too. And I have proof on my front porch that they are inquisitive and get into things before any of us know what's going on. That also ended up being one of their happiest evenings because you were there." His, too, but admitting that scared the blood right out of him.

For the first time since he'd got in the car, she grinned. "You do have a couple of great kids."

"On that we agree."

Taking a deep breath, she grew serious again. "Do you mind if I ask you a question?"

"I don't know. I mean you can ask, but I don't know if I'll answer." There was so much he couldn't tell her.

"What happened with their mother? Why don't you have any pictures?"

He instinctively pressed his lips tighter together. He didn't want to lie to her, but he couldn't tell her the truth either. They had been living in silence since Jessica's death. It was hard to switch gears and let any information out, even if it was false. She hated lies, and he was about to lie to her. His stomach twisted.

For the first time in three years, he had someone in his life he trusted with his girls, but he had to focus on their new lives. It hadn't been a challenge to stay low and not talk. But that was before Savannah. Acid rolled up his throat. "She died unexpectedly three years ago." Violently shot down in front of him. "We lost everything."

"I'm so sorry. Y'all were very close." She spoke so softly he barely heard her.

He nodded. "We were in our first year of college when we met. We planned on a long life together, well into retirement." They had had it all worked out on a spreadsheet. She had managed all the accounts. "We were supposed to be grandparents together." His skin tightened, and his gut clenched. Pressing his lips together again, he stopped talking. That was the most he had told anyone. It hurt not being able to talk about his wife.

The farm entrance came into view, and relief eased the tension in his shoulders. "I miss her every day, and I don't talk about it." That was the truth.

"I'm sorry. I know my mother had a hard time when she lost my father, but she had seven kids to raise. Looking back, I think some of her grief simply had to be pushed aside. I don't know how she did it. You're both very brave."

He needed to change the subject. "What about you? Why are you still single? Any great love in your life?"

Her arms were back in front of her, crossed over her midsection. "I thought there was, but it turned out I'm just a really bad judge of character. It was all lies. It's a horrible feeling, being used by people you thought loved you. I decided to come home and focus on building the business with my brother. Family might push me to my limits, but it's with good intentions. So no distractions—which means no relationships. I really need to focus on work."

She stared out the window, as if searching for something precious she had lost.

Did she think he was using her? Was he being selfish? He could never give her more than a friendship. A weak friendship at that.

Being in the witness protection program made loneliness his reality.

He leaned back against the headrest. This wasn't fair to her and made his life much more complicated. Maybe he should try again with another nanny. But the thought of that just drained him.

"You can drop me off at the barn. Reno's waiting for me. We'll swing by to pick up my truck on the way out."

It was on the tip of his tongue to invite her to dinner, but he bit back the words. In her current mood, she'd say no, and there was only so much rejection a man could take.

There was also the danger of losing his heart to a woman he wasn't allowed to give it to, even if she wanted it. It was a no-win situation. He should just let her go for both of their sakes.

Chapter Eight

Putting her phone away, she sighed. She'd been able to avoid Greyson and his girls for over a week. But with one call from him, she was on her way to the school again.

"Reno!" She called up to her brother in the loft without looking at him. He was going to love this, and she wasn't in the mood for his teasing. "Greyson called. There are problems in Rio Bella. He's going to be later than expected so I'm picking up the girls from school."

"Ha! And you said you're not the nanny? Okay." He was coming down the ladder.

"I told him no, but he doesn't know anyone else in town. I hate the thought of the girls being left at school." She had been forgotten once. Bridges had thought Margarita was picking her up, and her sister thought that their brother had her. It was horrible being the last kid in the pickup line. "He says he'll be here about an hour after school, so I can come back out and finish up a few things then."

Jumping down, he landed in front of her with an unusually serious expression. "Are you sure he's not interested in more than a nanny? He's been in town long enough to meet other people, and he seems like a nice guy, but he's not very open." He shrugged. "We don't know anything about him. Mom and the sisters all think you like him."

She rolled her eyes. "It's nothing like that. He still loves his wife. I'm an extra pair of hands to help with the girls. They're super sweet. He's been so busy with the farm that he hasn't had a chance to meet anyone else. I don't mind helping him."

He leaned back and crossed his arms. "You do like him."

"No." Throwing a rag at him, she glared at him. "It's not like that. The girls… Never mind. I'll be back at the barn around four thirty."

"Be careful, sis. I know you pretend that nothing bothers you, but you came home hurt. Greyson is a nice guy, but don't let him use you. Okay?"

She swallowed. That was her fear. That

Greyson was playing her. But she was doing this for the girls. "Those girls are the only reason I'm doing this. I know what it's like to lose a parent at their age. Plus, they're in a new town. That's it."

"I'm not buying it, but you're a grown-up, so we'll pretend you know what you're doing."

"Thanks." Her tone dripped sarcasm. "Have you heard any word on the supplies we ordered?"

"Yeah. While you go play nanny, I'm going to get the trailer and head over the hill. Peter texted a little while ago that everything was in and ready for pickup. You can help me unload in the morning. Tomorrow will be a long day, so don't worry about coming back to work tonight. Take an early one."

"How kind of you." She put her head down and went back to work. The hour went by too fast, and then it was time to get the girls.

She might have mixed emotions about Greyson, but the twins' ecstatic greeting when they saw her made her feel like a hero. Not wanting to sit in the long pickup line, she had parked a block over. She hugged the girls close as they talked over each other, telling her all about their day.

The teachers on afternoon duty all gave

her curious stares that made her skin itch. Guiding the girls to her truck, she made her escape as quickly as possible.

The girls talked nonstop all the way back to the farm. Going into the house, she noticed that the table was clear of boxes, but the formal living room still looked staged. Taking her by the hands, Abilene and Evelyn pulled her into the playroom, where the puppies greeted them with barks and tails wagging. Savannah wasn't sure which pair was more excited.

"Can we take our snack outside and play with Bliss and Finn?"

Snack? She had to feed them? "I had instructions to start you on your homework as soon as we got to the house."

Each had a wiggling pup licking their face. "We do, after we let the dogs outside and get a snack. Can we do our homework outside? It's nice out today."

"I guess. What do you usually eat?" She should text him, but really this sounded like something an adult watching children should be able to handle.

"Can we have popcorn? The bags are in the pantry, but Daddy doesn't want us to use the microwave by ourselves."

Popcorn. Her spine relaxed. "Yes. That's

something I can do." They went into the kitchen, and in short order had the popcorn in a bowl and glasses full of lemonade. Backpacks still on, they ran through the mudroom to the back door. She heard it open before she had time to follow with the popcorn and drinks. Finn and Bliss were fast on their heels.

"Girls, wait for me. Make sure you stay in my sight." The last time they'd gotten out of it, everyone ended up covered in mud.

Out of breath, she stepped onto the porch and stopped. The dogs were running along the fence and through the little flower beds, sniffing at everything as though it all was new. The girls' laughter made her smile.

Setting the bowl and glasses on the worn farmer's table, she took in the back porch. It was a large covered area. On one end stood a couple of rockers and an L-shaped couch, making for a cozy sitting area.

There was a group of different-sized lanterns on a cedar chest that acted as a coffee table. This was a whole other living space, and it might be her favorite. The only things missing were some throw blankets and pillows.

"Come eat while the dogs play." She had been given one job: to make sure they started their homework. She wasn't going to fail at this.

"It's so nice out here. Can we play longer before the sun goes down?" Evelyn said between sips of her drink.

Abilene nodded as she ate one white kernel at a time. "Being outside and playing is very important for brain development."

Grinning, Savannah tossed a few pieces into her mouth and eyed the twins. "I promised your dad you would get your homework done."

"We could do it out here," Abilene suggested.

"Please, please? Let us do it here on the porch."

"What classes do you have homework in?"

Grinning, they knew they had won. Setting their backpacks on the table, they pulled out folders. "We have math. And we need to practice our spelling words."

"Okay. I was always good at math, so if you need help, let me know."

She sat back and watched the sun paint the sky with the last colors of the day. The sound of birds and the breeze relaxed her more than she had thought possible while being alone with the girls.

"We're done with our math," Evelyn announced. "I'm going to the bathroom. When I come back, can you read our spelling words to us?"

"Sounds like a plan. I'll check your math work." She looked at her watch. It was past the time she had thought Greyson would be home. If it got much later, she was going to be responsible for dinner.

Her phone chimed. It was a text from Greyson. Taking longer than I anticipated. I'm picking up pizza.

A smile pulled at the corners of her mouth. It was as if he had heard her question. "Your dad is bringing pizza."

"Yay!" The girls cheered.

Her phone chimed again.

Sorry. I didn't ask your favorite pizza.

She responded, I love spinach, bacon and pineapple, but I'll eat anything you bring.

What would he think of her favorite combo? It grossed her brother out. Then she followed up with her one pizza rule.

Anything except for anchovies and onion. Everything else is a go for me.

But my favorite is anchovy. It's the only one the girls eat.

Then, I guess I'll become an anchovy lover.

You're too easy. Not even going to try and fight for your favorite?

She grinned. He had to be messing with her. She typed back, I'm easy to feed.

That's no fun, was his fast reply.

She couldn't stop the silly grin as she responded. I want to know who thought anchovies on pizza were a good idea.

Anchovy farmers trying to create a bigger market.

She laughed.

"What's funny?" Evelyn asked.

"Your dad is trying to make me an anchovy lover."

"Anchovy? What's that?" Abilene asked.

"He says it's your family's favorite pizza topping." Yeah, he had been messing with her.

Both girls looked confused. "No, it's not," Abilene said.

Evelyn shook her head. "Daddy's favorite is bacon with pineapple and lots of green spinach." She wrinkled her nose and stuck out her tongue. "We like pepperoni and cheese."

Abilene nodded. "His pizza is so weird."

Now she really had to laugh. "That's not weird at all. It's my favorite too."

Evelyn leaned forward. "You know what's really weird? Abilene loves pepperoni pizza, but she doesn't eat pepperoni. She takes them all off, then eats the cheese. Then she eats the crust last."

"That's not weird." Abilene glowered at her sister. "You're weird! You—"

"Girls." She pushed back her laughter. "That's enough. We're all a little weird. It's what makes us unique, even if we look alike." She gave the identical twins a side-eye. "I say keep it. Embrace it. Where are your spelling words?"

The temperature was dropping with the sun. "Let's get some blankets and pillows. We can sit on the couch and go over them."

Going up to their room, they pulled down a few blankets and a quilt, along with some soft pillows, then nestled in the corner of the outdoor sectional.

The two dogs had curled up with them. Word list finished, the girls had asked Savannah to read to them. This took her back to the early days with Reno.

That's how Greyson found them. She didn't notice him at first. But when she looked up, her heart, lungs and muscles stilled. He was leaning against the doorframe. The loneliness and longing that filled in his eyes was painful.

She was the wrong woman reading to his daughters. The pressure in her chest pushed inward. Forcing a deep breath, she made sure to relax her features.

"Look who's home," she whispered to the girls. Not to be quiet but because her throat wasn't working quite right.

"Daddy!" They jumped up and rushed to their father. With them gone, cold surrounded her.

It was a good reminder that this wasn't what she wanted. It wasn't. She needed to write that down and post it above her sink so she would see it every day. The one thing she knew without doubt. Greyson would never be the one to give it to her.

Greyson couldn't move when he first saw the perfect welcome-home bundled up on the back porch. This was what his girls craved.

His first response had been to smile at the gentle familial scene, but fear quickly chased it off, shredding any thought that he could have Savannah in his life.

He'd never be able to give them this. He had lost their mother. Not being able to protect her when she'd needed him most still kept him up at night.

It had been his job to protect and provide for her, and there hadn't been a morning that he hadn't felt up to the job. His business had been soaring, his wife was smart, beautiful and kind, and the twins were true gifts who knew nothing but joy. He'd had it all, and he'd never had a single doubt that he was in control of his world and could keep them all safe and happy.

But when he had held Jessica and watched the life fade from her eyes, he'd lost all his arrogant confidence.

Now he doubted everything. He was struggling to keep his daughters' hearts unbroken. But Savannah had stepped in and fixed things when he couldn't. She easily handed out the little touches and reassurances the twins needed.

His brain told him to run from this scene. That Savannah was dangerous to them all. But worse, that he was toxic for her. Being in the witness protection program, he couldn't offer her anything.

Even if he was free to love again, he knew that he would never have the faith to ask someone to share his life. The risk to her would be too great.

Taking a deep breath, he forced each muscle to relax. He started at his neck and worked his way down. Watching the trio, he leaned against the frame of the door and steadied his breathing.

His girls deserved this kind of warmth. He'd have to steel his heart to let Savannah into their lives, but if he could keep his distance, his girls could have these types of memories.

She glanced up, and her smile stirred his heart and beckoned him closer. The rush of feelings almost undid him. Lowering his head with a jerk, he broke eye contact and put his heart back in its box.

"Daddy!" The girls' joy reverberated across the porch.

Bringing his gaze back up to Savannah's, he saw the confusion in her expression, as well as perhaps hurt? Her eyes were so expressive. Her openly loving smile was gone.

"Join us, Daddy." Evelyn patted the cushion next to her, and Abilene snuggled closer to Savannah. "We're having so much fun out here."

He stayed where he was. "I can see that. Did you get all your homework done?"

"Yes. Savannah said we had to do it all before you got home. I beat Abby at spelling this time."

"Only by one." Abilene glared at her sister. Most of the time, the younger twin won any academic contest.

"I've got pizza in the kitchen," he interrupted before they fell into bickering. "Let's eat."

"Can we eat outside?"

Abilene nodded. "Please, Daddy? It'll be like a picnic. We did all our homework."

Savannah sat up a little straighter, a softer smile back in place as she looked at the girls. "You should go and eat the pizza. It's almost time to get ready for bed and past time for me to go home."

"Oh no," the girls said simultaneously as they clung to her. "Stay. We even have an extra room you can sleep in."

"Yes. Please. Please. We can have a sleepover!" Evelyn begged. "Right, Daddy?"

"No." Her laughter was soft. "I have to go home."

"No sleepovers, but I did promise pizza. I followed all the rules. Stay and eat with us." The house was warmer, calming, with her here.

"Yes! Yes! It'll be so much fun."

"It's a school night, so we won't be up too late," he warned the girls. "I know a couple of second graders who need to go to bed. I'll go get the pizza." He went back into the house without giving her a chance to turn down their dinner invitation.

There had to be a way to convince her that the girls needed her on some sort of regular schedule. She had said she couldn't do it because no one trusted her with kids. She had to see how much his girls loved her already. Maybe tonight would prove that? With the pizza in one hand and a bag with salad and flatware in the other, he headed back out to the porch.

Putting the two boxes on the table, he opened one of the lids. "So who's ready for anchovies and onions? Yum."

The girls scrambled off the sofa and came to the table. "Daddy, you're so silly." Evelyn opened the lid of the other pizza.

Abilene looked up at him. "Why did you lie to Savannah?"

For a moment the question stunned him, but she wasn't talking about his life. It was just the pizza. He placed his hand over his heart. "I did not lie." He exaggerated his words. "I thought you loved anchovies and onions."

"Savannah said anchovies are little fish." Abilene wrinkled her pert nose.

"Little fish on pizza is grosser than pineapple on pizza," Evelyn stated in a very grown-up-sounding voice.

"Daddy, do you know that Savannah's favorite pizza is also your favorite pizza? I didn't know anyone else liked pineapple and spinach on it. You could be girlfriend and boyfriend or something."

Horrified at what his daughter had just said, he glanced at Savannah. The shocked expression on her face made him laugh. So, she had no interest in him in that regard. That made it so much safer for her to spend more time with the girls.

He didn't have the confidence or the heart to ever be in another relationship, but everyone in town seemed to have a different idea.

He lowered his chin and gave her a pointed stare. "You don't have to look so horrified. My feelings are hurt, Savannah." Grinning, he pulled out the chair and sat. "Let's eat, and then you can go home. You don't have to worry about me and any dishonorable intentions."

Putting a slice of pepperoni pizza on her plate, Evelyn looked up at him. "What does *dishonorable intentions* mean?" she asked, sounding out the new words.

With a sigh, he shook his head. Thinking ahead before he spoke in front of the twins would be a good habit to develop. His girls were too quick to pick up on things they shouldn't. "It means to have bad plans for someone. I'm pretty sure Savannah does not want to be my girlfriend. And I'm not trying to find one either."

"It would be cool if you had a girlfriend. Farmers should have wives, and you can't get a wife if you don't have a girlfriend. Savannah would make a really great girlfriend. And she would make a great mother." Abilene had laid it out.

Evelyn nodded. "It would be nice to have a mother."

His chest tightened. They had a mother. He swallowed the slam of grief down and tried to breathe normally.

"Oh, sweetheart." Savannah reached over and kissed the top of her head. "You have a mother. Just like I still have a father. They just can't be here with us in person. But they are in our hearts always. She loved you very much, and she will always love you, even in heaven."

"Yes," he croaked out. "Your mother does love you. I'm so sorry she can't be here with you."

"Oh, Daddy. We love Mommy. We know she's here in our hearts. We meant it would be

nice to have Savannah around like a mother."
The girls looked crestfallen. Once again, he'd
sucked all the joy out of the room.

"Savannah does make a great friend.
Friends can hang out and have a good time.
We don't have to be boyfriend and girlfriend
to do that. And I'm not getting married again.
You can't say things like that to people."

They both nodded, giving him a tentative
smile. "But, Daddy, why would you have
to tell Savannah that you don't have bad
thoughts?" Evelyn still looked way too serious.

"It was a joke." He needed to get them off
this line of thought. But maybe he could use
it to lay the groundwork for convincing Savannah of his plan. "Neither one of you has
touched the salad. You need to make sure to
eat some greens and fiber."

With a few grumbles, the girls each put
some salad onto their plates and added dress-
ing. Then they told him about the stories
they'd read and went into the details of their
day and of Savannah picking them up in the
truck. How Savannah let them bring the dogs
to the backyard to play. How Savannah loved
doing her homework outside when she was
little. Savannah was in every sentence.

She didn't say much. Keeping her attention on the girls, she smiled and nodded. Occasionally, she would send him an uncertain look, and he smiled back. If they kept their focus on the girls, he could do this. When they were done with their stories of the day and their dinner, he sent them inside to go take a bath.

Savannah started gathering up the paper plates. "The girls were great. Thank you for trusting me with them again. But I should stop while I'm ahead. It's time for me to head home. Tell them good-night for me."

"They'll be upset if you leave without saying goodbye." He tried to think of the right words to get her to agree to help him with the twins. "I can't tell you how much I appreciate this. I have a hard time trusting people with my girls. Hopefully there won't be any more last-minute emergencies."

She chuckled. "If there is one guarantee in life, it's that there will always be emergencies and ruined plans."

Did she not see how essential she had become in his daughters' lives?

For the first time since he'd taken his family into hiding, he had someone he wanted to tell the truth to. But he couldn't. What could he tell her to keep her involved with his family?

"You know, this might be hard to understand, but in a short time you've become family to Evelyn and Abilene. That's something they haven't had in their short memories. Even having your mother over here the other night was special for them. At church, your family just embraced them. For the first time in a long time, they feel like they belong somewhere. Here in Port Del Mar, because of your family's welcome. That's all due to you."

She stopped being busy and went still. "My family is pretty remarkable." Lips between her teeth, she looked up at him. Blinked a couple of times. "They aren't anywhere close to perfect, but I wouldn't trade them for anything. I'm glad they've helped your girls."

"As great as your family is, Savannah, it's you. You've done that for them." He broke eye contact and looked out over the porch. Savannah had made this a little sanctuary in one short evening. She didn't seem to know how amazing she was.

"I haven't done anything my mom or sisters wouldn't do for you if you asked." She gave a dry chuckle. "Anything good you see in me comes from them. They're big, loud and in your face trying to take care of everyone. I can't imagine my life without them. I do thank God for my family...most nights. But your girls have family. They have you."

With a heavy sigh, she sat down and stared into the night sky. The last glow of the sun slipped down below the horizon. The café lights he had strung along the columns of the porch surrounded her. The gentle curves of her face were highlighted in the soft glow.

She was so beautiful, but he heard what she didn't say. In the middle of her big loving family, she was alone. The desire to pull her close nudged him, but he couldn't. Not as long has he had to lie to her about who he was.

They sat in silence for a while, him studying her, her studying the night sky. She was so good with all three of them. She deserved a man in her life who could love her completely and protect her the way he couldn't protect Jessica.

His poor girls were stuck with him, but Savannah had so many options, and they were all better than him. There was no way he'd let another woman down.

She turned to him. "I'm glad my family could help even a little, but you're the one holding your family together. Being with you and the twins has made me even more aware of the sacrifices my mom made raising seven kids on her own."

Her chin tilted down as she studied the porch steps. "It's hard losing a parent. But I can only imagine how hard it is losing a partner. I might question your judgment—" she gave him a half-hearted smile "—but I'll always answer your call. Those girls already own a piece of my heart."

His heart hit a double beat. This was it. He'd ask her now, and she'd say yes. It was for the girls. He would make that clear. Nothing personal between them.

"The girls are fond of you as well. We—" He swallowed back the words. "I mean *they*. They need you. You've brought something to them that I can't. I don't know how. Jess—" Oh man. His wife's name hadn't passed his lips in so long. Closing his eyes, he took a settling breath. "Sorry. Just the other day, I was trying to figure out how I was going to get the farm operating and make sure the girls don't feel forgotten."

He moved closer to her but kept his attention on the dark sky. "My wife always said parenting was a team sport. I never understood until I lost her and..." Why was he stumbling over words and struggling with keeping to his new backstory? "What I want to say is that the girls wouldn't be as happy as they are right now if you hadn't stepped onto our porch that day."

"Greyson." She placed a hand on his arm. He wanted to lean into the warmth, but he forced himself to step back.

With a couple of confused blinks, she stuffed her hand into her jacket pockets. "You're a great father. I see how hard you work to keep everything balanced. You're right, we're not meant to do it alone."

He nodded. "I've given it a lot of thought, and I want to offer you a legitimate business deal helping with the girls. No lying, no pretending to date. A real schedule so that we can plan for you to have time with them, and I know on those nights I can get extra work done."

Bracing his hands on the railing, he took a few deep breaths. This was for his children. He could keep his distance. He shifted and rubbed the back of his neck. "Spring break is coming. I've been able to move most of my appointments and jobs around to free up time, but there're a few days that I'll need help. I know you're working hard on the barns. It's okay if they get pushed back. The girls are the most important thing to me."

Turning, he crossed his arms over his chest and leaned a hip against the railing.

The nighttime sounds surrounded them. If he thought begging would help, he'd drop to his knees right now, but she deserved some time to think about it.

No. No. No. No. The word was easy. She opened her mouth to say it. Two little letters, but so much power. The power was hers. *Say* no.

Turning him down was the right thing to do. Feelings she had vowed to keep locked away until she was standing on her own two feet were tickling her heart. But the fluttering had nothing to do with the twins. She was developing feelings for *him*, the dangerous kind. There were too many red flags.

He was hiding something. For some reason, he was holding back information—or maybe he was outright lying to her.

She couldn't trust herself—or him. Taking a deep breath, she looked up into the stars. Her answer had to be *no*. But the girls needed her.

God, Mom tells me to trust You. But how do I know if these feelings are from You?

Her gaze went to the back door, where the girls had disappeared inside. The window was glowing with a warm light. It beckoned her to come in, as if she belonged here.

For the first time in her life, someone truly needed her. Not her family or the connections she could get them. They just wanted her. The girls did, anyway. They made her heart happy in an unexpected way. Greyson's motives were not as clear.

It was nice being important to them in a way she had never been to anyone else. Dragging her gaze from the house, she turned to Greyson. He was casually leaning against the railing as if her responses didn't really matter, but she knew they did.

His cool green eyes had storms lurking in them. Her saying *yes* was important to him because of the twins. She wasn't important enough to get the real him. That, she knew deep in her bones, was well hidden, and he was going to keep it that way.

It might be her overly active imagination, but her gut told her that Greyson needed her too. So what made this man different from everyone else? Maybe it was just wishful thinking. Of course, that same intuition had told her that Colin had needed her.

Keeping her gaze on the Big Dipper, she tried to ignore his closeness as he sat down next to her. "I trusted people I shouldn't have. The man I loved lied to me about his name.

I came home feeling like a fool. It proved I have horrible judgment all around."

He was silent for a moment. "We've all made mistakes. I get that. You're still the best person to spend time with my kids."

"But I'm not. My poor judgment has a long history. It started when Reno was four and *I* lost him at the beach." Her stomach clenched at the memory. "He was gone for sixteen hours. Everyone thought the worst. My father kept asking me where I last saw him. My mother cried as everyone frantically searched. My older siblings yelled at me. They couldn't believe I had let him play hide-and-seek at the beach. It had been a bad decision. The hours he was missing were a nightmare I relive all the time. He was my responsibility, and we all thought he was dead. Then one of the fishing boats came in, and they discovered him hiding. He was there the whole time they were out to sea, hiding in a small box."

He moved closer, his hand resting on her forearm. "He was safe. It was a game of hide-and-seek that went wrong. But he's here today, and everything's fine. What does this have to do with the boyfriend that lied to you?"

"They're just two examples that show I have a long history of making bad decisions.

I haven't outgrown it or gotten any smarter. I thought when I left town I would prove myself. But it just reinforced that I can't make good decisions on my own. My art mentor? I thought she hung the moon. They needed money, I just handed it over. I had a boyfriend I thought loved me."

Her throat closed at all the pain and humiliation resurfacing. Even after a year, it hurt how wrong she had been about everything. "Have you ever had a time in your life that was so good you wonder how life can get any better? But then it all blows up in a huge, out-of-control fire?"

He reached out and took her hand. The warmth traveled through her, making her want to lean against him. She forced herself to sit, letting her hand stay in his.

"Yeah. It would be safe to say I know the feeling. I'm sorry. I wouldn't wish that on anyone. But you must know that you're a good person. That's what made it easy for them to use you. You see the best in others. It's not a bad trait, and it doesn't make you irresponsible or flighty. It makes you a person who cares about others. Like you care for my girls."

"It doesn't make me feel like a good person. I feel like an idiot." She rubbed her temples. "I really do care for your girls, but I feel like I don't know you at all. I can't shake the feeling that you are lying to me about something."

He stood and stepped off the porch. "You know the important stuff."

She waited, hoping he would trust her enough to say more. Why was there so much no one knew about him?

"I love my children. They're all I have left of my wife. I moved here to give us a fresh start. I want to build new memories. After the tragedy we lived through, they deserve a happy childhood, one free from fear and sadness. I love working outdoors with plants. I always have. I'm new to farming, and it's much more overwhelming than I had imagined, and for the first time in my life I worry I can't make it work. My girls and the farm. That's all there is to know about me. I also don't like asking for help."

He turned and moved to stand in front of her. Sitting on the top step, she was almost eye to eye with him. For a long moment, they stared at each other as he searched her face. "I'm asking you for help because I trust you with the most precious part of my life."

"Greyson." She shook her head. Her throat was dry. "Everyone in town, including my family, will tell you that I'm not the person for this."

"Then, they don't know you. You were a kid yourself when your brother snuck onto a boat and disappeared for hours. I know it must have been terrifying, but you're remembering it from a child's confused perspective. Everyone you looked up to was scared. It had to be terrifying. On your own for the first time, you trusted the wrong people. I've been there. At one point most of us have. It has nothing to do with you being a good person. That's what you are, a good person. A person I trust with my daughters. The only one I trust. I'm not asking for a full-time commitment. Two days during spring break and one day a week after school. You don't have to trust me or do anything with me. It's for them. Will you help us?"

Oh, he was not playing fair. It was at moments like this that she was in danger of losing her heart to a man she didn't really know. She had poured out her darkest secrets. He hadn't run, but she'd noticed he didn't share any of his own.

Could she watch the twins and keep him at a distance? She closed her eyes. *God, did You put him and his girls in my path for a reason? Am I supposed to walk away, or say yes?*

"Savannah?"

Opening her eyes, she met his gaze. "I need to pray about this. I don't want to say no to your girls, but I have a plan, and this is not part of that plan. Can I give you an answer tomorrow?"

"I'm not asking anyone else, so you have a few days to think about it. Can you let me know Sunday, at church?"

She nodded. The girls came to the back door, saving her from saying anything else to him. They wrapped their arms around her when she told them she was leaving.

"Stay! We have an extra bed."

"Girls, if you don't let her go, she might not come back."

"Oh no. You must come back. We have books to finish."

"Daddy says we can go to the beach during spring break. Will you come with us?"

"Um, I don't do the beach. Haven't gone in years... All the sand. Yuck."

The girls both pouted. "But everyone loves the beach. We want to build sandcastles."

"I'm sure you'll have a great time. I need to go now. Have a good night." She hugged each girl and kissed them on their foreheads.

Greyson followed her out to the front door.

"You haven't been back to the beach since Reno was a stowaway."

She grinned. That was the first time she had been able to smile when thinking of that day. "A *stowaway*? No one's ever put it like that. My parents tried to take me back a couple of times with the family. I cried the whole time, and they finally gave up."

"Maybe it's time to try and make some new memories. That's why I'm here. Help us…my girls make those memories."

"I can't. I might watch the girls, but I will not take them to the beach. That's too much."

Driving home, she prayed. By the time she had pulled into the driveway, she knew she would be watching the twins. She also had a bad feeling that God thought it was a great time for her to go back to the beach.

Chapter Nine

The following day, she told Greyson she'd help him over spring break, but that she would not take the girls to the beach alone. Plus, she hated crowds, and their small town became a destination during spring break. She told him that she'd talk to the girls about alternate activities when she had them that could be just as fun.

But, as usual, her plans were derailed. The very next day, Josefina called. Belle De La Rosa had invited them out for the day to her private beach on the ranch.

One of Belle's daughters was in class with the twins and wanted to invite them too. It was a personal invitation to a private beach from someone who would make a good friend for the girls. This was what they wanted. A day at the beach and a chance to make new friends outside of school. There was no way she could say no.

Her sister had told her that, along with Belle, a couple of the De La Rosa wives would also be there with their children. Josefina didn't want her to worry about being alone at the beach with the girls. She had made sure to tell her that lots of other moms who were good with children would be there.

Relief and resentment swam in circles around her gut. The lack of trust her sister still had in her hurt. But she was also reassured that they would be with a small group that would help watch the girls. Extra eyes, and all that.

Taking a deep breath, she let the warring emotions go. *God, I know You got this. You put this in my path for a reason, so I'm trusting You.*

In the back seat, both girls had their faces pressed to the windows with anticipation. Excitement bounced off them. Bliss and Finn sat in their laps, tails wagging.

"I thought we were going to the beach?" Evelyn said, as they drove through the De La Rosa ranch past pastures of cattle and horses.

"We are. It's a special beach that no one else gets to go to. Not many people are invited out here to this location. At certain times of the year, the turtles come here to lay their eggs, so it's not open to the public."

Abilene gasped. "Turtles lay eggs? Like birds? How did I not know that?"

"Are we gonna get to hunt turtle eggs? Do they build nests?" Evelyn looked way too excited.

Savannah laughed. "No. They start coming next month, and we don't hunt the turtle eggs. They're an endangered species. I'm sure you'll learn about them in school, since this is one of the few places in the world where they lay their eggs." Crossing a cattle guard, she guided her truck between two large sand dunes covered in grass and wild sunflowers. "Are you ready for this?"

She eased past the dunes, and on the other side the horizon opened to the endless view of the Gulf of Mexico.

At first, the girls just stared, mouths open. Then they clapped and bounced in their seats. "It's the beach!"

They started chatting about all the things they wanted to do and see. Savannah scanned the area for signs of Belle or Josefina. They were supposed to meet them here on the beach, but she didn't see anyone.

She glanced at the time. They had said ten o'clock, and it was five to ten. That shouldn't

count as early, but ranch life could be unpredictable. And her sister was always about ten
to fifteen minutes late to this sort of thing.

"Okay. It looks like we're the first ones here.
We'll park by the dunes and walk in since we
don't want to drive on the beach." Pulling the
truck to the side, she got out, then helped the
girls with their beach bags and the dogs.

"Stay close to me. Don't go off anywhere."
Her stomach hurt at the thought of being here
alone with the children. But she could do this.
Making them sit in the truck until someone
else showed up would be ridiculous.

Once everyone arrived, she'd feel better.
Her fear wasn't rational but being on the
beach alone with minors made her mind want
to play the worst what-if scenarios.

Finn and Bliss ran into a flock of seagulls,
barking as the birds scattered. She might have
more to worry about with the dogs than the
girls.

"Put the leashes on them."

"They've never been to the beach either."
Abilene laughed.

"Can we go to the edge where the waves
are?" Evelyn called for the dogs, and both
came back to them. "See? They'll stay with
us."

Pulling the blanket out of her oversize bag,

Savannah said, "The sun will be brutal after an hour, so I have a canopy in the back of my truck. Y'all will need a break from the sun. Here." She handed them bottles of water from the small ice chest she'd brought. "Stay close to the blanket for now and drink these. I'm going to get the canopy. Once it's up, we'll go wade in the water." Hopefully by then someone else would be here.

Taking the water bottles, the girls sat on the edge of the blanket and opened their backpacks. They pulled out the castle-building paraphernalia Greyson had bought them and stacked it on the blanket.

Savannah reached into her pocket for her phone to let Greyson know they had arrived and to check whether there was a message from one of the De La Rosas or her sister. But her phone wasn't there.

It wasn't in the bag. She must have left it in the truck. The girls were already digging and making a pile of sand on one edge of their little hole. Did they need another layer of sunblock?

"I need to go to the truck to get my phone and the canopy. Stay right there. Don't move, okay?"

The girls nodded, barely looking up at her. She took a deep breath. Really, she was just walking to the truck. There was no reason for her heart to be beating so fast. *Just breathe. It's okay. Be normal.*

She chuckled at herself. Being normal was never her strong suit.

Glancing at the girls, she smiled. Abilene was standing over their mound as Evelyn handed her a bucket full of sand. The dogs jumped at the sand the girls poured.

She reached for the extra beach bag and glanced inside for her phone. Nope, not there. It had fallen out somewhere in the back seat. She checked on the girls. They were both standing now and molding their pile of sand with shovels, engrossed in their sandcastle.

Going to the back of the truck, she yanked the blue canopy out and propped it on the side, then went to the back seat and dug around for her phone. She bent over to look under the seat. It wasn't there.

She twisted to the other side and dug through the disorder underneath the back bench. Cables, wrenches and other unidentifiable objects cluttered the area. It was way past time to clean out her truck and organize it.

Stretching across the bench seat, her hand touched something smooth and sleek. She fished around, but she couldn't quite grab it. Lying on her stomach, her feet now off the ground, she finally managed to pull it to her. She looked down for messages. There was one from Greyson, and a missed call.

She hit the button.

"Hey. I missed your call. Everything okay?"

"Yep. I finished early and left the guys in charge so I'm joining you. I'm at the ranch gate. I wasn't sure if I could manage it, so I didn't want to disappoint you or the girls by saying I'd be there and then not. I know how hard this is for you emotionally. How's everything going?"

"It's good. I'm good." That he was worried about her melted her heart a little bit. "We just got here. The girls will be so excited when they see you." She scooted back. With a grin on her face, she got to her feet and straightened. She closed the door with her hip and lifted the canopy by the handle at the end. "I'm setting up the canopy to give them a break from the sun."

"Good idea."

She pulled hard. It might be easier to just carry the thing. "It has wheels, but I'm guessing they weren't designed for sand."

He laughed. Smiling, she turned around to join the girls.

They weren't there. The blanket was empty. The half-formed castle abandoned.

She scanned the beach. Not a single sign of them. How could they have gotten away from her?

"I don't see the girls." Her heart was in her throat. Everything was clamming up. She couldn't breathe. Couldn't move.

No. She wouldn't allow herself to panic. They were here, and they needed her to be clearheaded.

"What do you mean, you don't see them?"

Dropping the canopy, Savannah ran to the spot where she had left them. "They were digging in the sand. I went to get my phone out of the truck. It was a few minutes."

A dog barked. She looked farther down to the left. The jetty. Barking, Bliss ran between the two triangular man-made rock formations that reached out into the gulf. The dog stopped and looked over at her before turning to look back down below the pile of huge boulders, weighing several tons each.

Savannah took off running. At the edge of the first red boulders, she fell to her knees. At the base of the jetty the girls stood on a very narrow strip of sand. Abilene clung to a wet Finn. The tide was coming in, and the waves were hitting the end of the jetty hard, spraying water.

"Savannah!" Evelyn waved. She said something else, but then a wave hit and covered every other sound.

"Savannah? What's going on? Where are the girls?" Greyson's voice helped her focus.

"They're below the jetty. Everyone is fine, but the boulders are too tall for them to climb back up. I'm going to get them." She dropped her phone. The crashing waves were so loud she was sure the girls couldn't hear her.

Abilene started crying, and Finn licked her face. Another hard wave splashed against the rock closer to the girls, sending sprays of water over them. One of those waves could sweep the girls out and pull them under.

No. God, You have us. I'm here, and I'll get them out. She started maneuvering over the rocks to reach them. Smaller rocks filled the cracks and crevices between the jagged red boulders.

Evelyn was trying to climb up one of the big rocks, but she couldn't quite reach the top of it. "Savannah! Finn chased a crab down here and got trapped." Another wave cut her off.

"I'm coming. Just hold on."

Wet, the giant rocks were hard to maneuver around. "It's going to be all right." Prayers had never come so hard and heavy in her adult life. She smiled, hoping to keep the twins calm.

Abilene hugged Finn close to her. "But the rocks are too big for us to climb up. They're all wet and slippery."

"Just stay as close to the rocks as you can." The waves seem to be getting bigger.

"The water burns my eyes," Evelyn said, sliding back down from the boulder she was attempting to climb.

"It's salt water, sweetheart." She was halfway down. How had they gotten so far away so quickly? "Hang on, girls. I'm coming, and your dad is on his way."

"Oh, Daddy's going to be so mad. You told us to put their leashes on and stay by the blanket." Abilene started crying again, and Evelyn wrapped her arms around her.

"He wants you safe." *Really, God, was this what You wanted for me?* Only able to move over one rock at a time was taking her forever. She hated the helplessness.

A smaller rock wiggled under her, and she stopped. If it rolled away, it could hit the girls. Even the smallest ones could do damage. Reaching over, she found a secure rock, then dropped down to the sandy, flat area where the twins stood.

They rushed to her, throwing their arms

around her. The waves rolled in, bringing the water above her ankles. Another hit too quickly. It was bigger than the previous ones. She pulled the girls close and leaned against the rocks. The harshness of the waves stung her skin. It was official: she hated the beach.

Waves were fun to look at from a distance. But standing amid such a force of nature crashing against the rocks was terrifying. They needed to get out of here. "I'm going to lift Abilene up first. Let Finn go. I'll put him on the top of this big rock, and he can climb the rest of the way up."

Abilene shook her head. "That's why we came down here. He was stuck. We can't leave him."

"We won't leave him, sweetheart." She took Finn and lifted him over the huge boulders at the base. He started scrambling up, but then stopped halfway and looked back at them. "See, he's waiting for you, Abilene. Once you get up, I'll lift Evelyn."

"But what about you?"

Another wave hit, and it pulled at her legs. "I'm taller." She lifted the twin in her arms, then placed her hands under the small feet to give her another push upward. "It's slippery. Be careful and take it one rock at a time. Can you get to the next rock above?"

Abilene reached and pulled herself up. Looking back down at them, she nodded.

"Good job, Abby. You're doing it." Evelyn cheered on her sister.

Bliss disappeared, then reappeared followed by Belle and Josefina. Savannah wanted to cry all over again. Relief flooded her. The girls wouldn't be alone as she tried to climb out.

The other women reached for Abilene and pulled her to the top. One twin was safe. They asked her something, but with the waves roaring around them, she couldn't hear the words.

She turned to Evelyn. "Okay. Your turn." Cupping her hands together, she heaved Evelyn high enough to get over the bottom boulder.

The waves were hitting harder and higher on her legs. Evelyn was almost to the top. They would be safe. Now she had to find a way over the six-foot rocks at the base.

The sea settled a little, and Belle cupped her hands around her mouth. "I'll be right back," she yelled, then disappeared. Josefina lay down on her belly and reached down for Evelyn. "She's got some rope and some other equipment in her truck. We'll get you outta there."

Savannah's knees went weak with relief.

Sagging against the boulder, seaweed made it too slick for her to get a firm grip. The girls were safe. Of course, her sister was here to see what a mess she'd made of watching them. Before dinner was served tonight, her whole family would know how she'd managed to ruin another day on the beach.

Water slammed into her back and pulled at her legs, reminding her that she was running out of time.

"Savannah, can you get on the top of the boulder?" her sister shouted.

Could she? With all the force that she could muster, she pulled herself up, but she lost her grip and her footing slipped. Taking a deep breath, she eyed her target. Jumping, she reached up as high as she could and managed to get a grip in a crevice. She pulled. The labor of woodworking paid off with the upper strength she'd developed. Her top half was over the boulder.

"You've got it! You can do it." Voices from the top of the jetty cheered her on.

Eyes closed and jaw locked with determination, she pulled herself up to the biggest boulder. If she reached that spot, she'd be safe from being sucked out into the gulf by the fierce waves. One of the rocks shifted under her weight, then rolled.

She froze. After a minute, she found new footing, then lunged and reached the top of the biggest boulder.

Falling forward, she took a moment to catch her breath. She'd done it. The only problem was that now her arms shook, and her fingertips were raw.

"Savannah? Are you okay? Answer me." Greyson's voice was hard.

She waved as she turned herself over to look up at the small audience above her. He was here. Everything was going to be okay.

"I'm fine. I just need to catch my breath."

"Not sure how much time you have." Greyson wasn't looking at her, but out to the ocean at the waves coming in. The little piece of beach the girls had been standing on was underwater.

He took off his jacket. "I'm coming down to get you." Why was he wearing a suit at the beach?

"No. I can get myself up. You're not going to ruin another work outfit because of me." Taking a deep breath, she closed her eyes and focused all her strength.

One, two, three. Reaching high, she pulled with her arms as she pushed from her feet. Stepping up, she found another place for her foot. One movement at a time, she carefully found a thin crack between the boulders that gave her leverage to move upward. Her muscles shook with the strain.

"You're doing it, Savannah. You're almost here," the twins cheered her on. Despite being tired, cold and wet, she had to smile.

Greyson was easing down with a rope Belle had given him.

"Just a couple more steps and you have it." That was her sister's voice.

With a nod and her gaze locked on Greyson, she reached out and got a new foothold. As she pushed against it, the rock slipped out from under her, and another was dislodged. She watched in slow motion as it pinned her lower leg.

There was a snap, followed by excruciating pain.

She tried to bite her lip to stop any noise from coming out, but she wasn't successful.

"Savannah! Don't move." Greyson was close, but she had her eyes tightly closed.

Dropping her chin to her chest, she fought for control with deep, slow breaths. Opening her eyes, she looked down and knew she was in trouble. She wanted to point out that there was no way for her to move unless she could roll the hundred-pound rock off her leg. But she couldn't speak.

"I'm coming in on your left."

With the way she was turned, he was coming in behind her.

It took everything she had not to cry or yell or scream. Or any combination of all three. But everyone was watching.

This was the worst pain she'd ever felt in her life. Her vision blurred, and her stomach rolled. She laid her head against the wet cold rock and worked hard to stay awake. If she passed out, she'd be deadweight and would put them both in danger.

Greyson's arm came around her from behind. "You win. I'm never making you come to the beach again."

A snort escaped her throat. "You think you're funny?" She did feel better, just having him close.

A rope was going under her arms. "Savannah, I know you hate being rescued, but I don't think you're getting out of this one alone."

She nodded in agreement. Greyson moved around and put his foot on the rock that had her leg pinned.

"If I lift the rock, can you go up? Do you have the strength to move quickly?"

"I will." What else was she going to do? Giving up was not allowed in the Espinoza family. And in that she was just like the rest of them. She couldn't allow him to dislodge the rock *and* carry her out of this mess.

"I'll count and have them pull you up as soon as I know I can hold the rock off your leg. Ladies, can you hear me?"

Belle gave a thumbs-up.

"Good. When I say *now*, pull the rope and push with your free leg."

Another thumbs-up, and the three women took positions to pull as one. There were so many things that could go wrong, and they all knew it, but Savannah trusted Greyson not to let anything hurt her.

"I'm going to give you a count. Move out of the way as fast as you can. I don't know how long I can hold it. Are you ready?" He looked her in the eye.

She nodded.

"One. Two. Three." He grunted.

She pulled her leg free, the pain causing her stomach to heave.

"Now!" he yelled, and the rope was pulled, lifting her up. When she opened her eyes, she was looking up at the sky and soft sand was at her back. Had she blacked out?

For a moment she just lay there, looking at the sky and trying to regulate her breathing. Blue, clear, beautiful. All the kids and the women formed a semicircle, looking down at her. Her tribe. "Where's Greyson?" She couldn't breathe until she knew he was safe.

She shifted to look down. Her shoe was gone, and there was blood. Then she saw her leg.

She jerked her gaze to the sky. To say it was broken would be an understatement.

Greyson was on his knee next to Belle, who was kneeling over her leg. Savannah trusted her. She had emergency medical training. Biting her bottom lip so she wouldn't get sick, she took deep breaths to ease her stomach.

People were talking to her. The twins got right in her face, but she couldn't hear them. They had to be upset. She tried to say something to reassure them but didn't know if she was successful. Her sight blurred.

"I'm so sorry." Belle used her professional voice. That scared Savannah like nothing else had. "I know you're in pain. We need to stop the bleeding and stabilize your leg." She kept talking, but Savannah couldn't hear her. Everything went black.

When she opened her eyes again, she was lying across the bench seat of Greyson's SUV. Her foot was propped up.

A car door shut. Her lips would probably bleed from biting down on them, but she refused to be sick in Greyson's car. She had already made too many messes in his life.

"Get her there as soon as possible, but also safely." Belle was at the front window, talking to Greyson. He was pulling his seat belt on. "Rushing and tossing her around could make it worse. I'm so sorry these roads are rough." Belle backed away.

Greyson didn't waste time getting to the road. "I'll try and take it easy. I know you're in pain. You were incredible today. I'm sorry I wasn't there sooner."

"The girls?" Her fist clenched against the pain.

"They're with your sister. Thanks to you, they're safe. The tide came in fast. If you had waited for help, it might have been too late."

She shook her head. He shouldn't be thanking her. It was all her fault. But she couldn't talk about it right now. It took all of her energy to hold herself together.

Chapter Ten

His elbows braced on his knees, Greyson dug his fingers through his hair. The surgery to repair Savannah's leg had taken longer than they had predicted, and there had been complications.

She'd had a bad reaction to the anesthetic. Yolanda had refused to leave her side once they'd gotten her into a room. For the first time since he'd driven her from the beach, he was alone with Savannah.

Resa had taken their mother to get something to eat, and Reno was on his way back up. Every member of her family and some friends had been taking turns sitting with her mother by Savannah's bedside.

Every time he'd been in the room, she'd been asleep. Her family had spoken with her and assured him she was in a good mood, all things considered.

For some reason, he didn't trust that report. He knew they were telling him the truth, but he also knew how upset she must be at the whole situation. She hadn't wanted to be responsible for his children. She hadn't even wanted to go to the beach. But in both cases, he had pushed her until she couldn't say no. In his stupid pride, he had thought she needed to do those things.

He had serious doubts she was being honest with her family. As close as they were, she was always protecting them and never let them see her down.

In his gut, he knew she blamed herself. He was here to make sure she knew how grateful he was for her actions. More than grateful. He loved her. Not that he could let her know that.

He dropped his head. When he had seen her at the base of the jetty, his heart had stopped. She was in danger, and he hadn't known if he could get her out. The nightmare of losing her like he had lost Jessica kept him awake at night.

A soft groan from the bed brought his head up. Her mocha-brown eyes blinked a couple of times.

He immediately stood and went to her bedside, reaching out for her hand. He made sure to avoid all the tubes and needles. He craved feeling her warm skin, her pulse, the proof of life.

"Greyson?" Her voice sounded rough.

"Hey. It's good to see you awake." He gently squeezed her wrist and smiled. "The girls made me bring thank-you cards and flowers." With a half smile he scanned the bright colors filling her room. "If flowers are a sign of love, then you are very much loved." He waved at the oversize bouquet of yellow and purple flowers. "Here's our offering of love."

Once the word slipped out, his throat went dry. *Love* was not a word he could throw around. What was wrong with him? He cleared his throat of the sudden dryness that threatened to choke him.

"Anyway. It's from the girls. They picked it out. I…we wanted to tell you how much… um…we appreciate everything you've done for the girls. You've gone way beyond the call of duty."

She shook her head. "Stop. We both know they were in danger because of me."

He frowned at her. This was exactly what he'd feared. "We know no such thing. I'm the one that pushed you to go. They told me they didn't follow your directions. And believe me, they feel so guilty I can barely get them to eat." He sighed. Pulling the chair closer to the bed, he sat down and leaned forward. "I'm here to talk about you. How are you doing?"

She smiled and started to say something, but he cut her off.

"No. How are you really doing? I know you well enough to know the smiles you're giving your family are a cover-up, so *they* feel better." He moved into her space until they were inches apart. "What are you worrying about, and how can I help?"

The need to do something to fix this was so strong that he was restless with the lack of action. He searched her eyes.

After a moment of eye contact, she turned her head to the side and stared at the bathroom door.

"Savannah, you didn't do anything wrong. This is not your fault. You risked yourself to get my girls to safety. Please tell me what I can do for you."

She sucked her top lip between her teeth. Unshed tears made her eyes glisten. She shook her head, but she didn't say a word. Her breathing became labored.

He braced an arm on the side of her bed. He gently touched her face and brought her gaze back to his. "Please, tell me what's going on in that beautiful head of yours." Not sure why he was so desperate for her to tell him the truth, he took a deep breath and tried to give her space. "Please, Savannah." Now he was pleading.

Glancing down, she gently laced her bandaged fingers through his and squeezed. "I had told them to put leashes on the dogs, but I didn't make sure it was done. I should never have gone back to the truck and left them alone. How can you look at me?"

"No, it wasn't your fault." He placed his finger under her chin and gently lifted it, but she lowered her lashes, hiding from him. "Savannah, look at me please."

She finally shifted her gaze to his. The tears in her eyes drove a knife through his heart. "It's not your fault," he whispered as he laid his forehead against hers. "Please. You're breaking my heart."

"The truck was in your line of sight. You didn't do anything I haven't done a million times. If that had been me, would you think it was my fault?"

This beautiful, wild girl had snuck into his heart. He hadn't known he had enough heart left for someone other than his children. The instinct to fix this for her was stronger than it had ever been. But this wasn't about him. He was doing this for his daughters and Savannah.

"The girls love you, and they feel horrible about what happened. I owe you so much."

"Please tell them I'm not mad. I'm in the habit of blaming myself. So thank you for your kind words." She used her free hand to wipe at the tears on her face. "I hate crying."

With his thumb, he took care of the side of her face she couldn't reach. "The girls promise to be better listeners. The cards they made include apologies. And I didn't even have to tell them to do that."

"That's very sweet of them, but it's more than what happened at the beach." She sighed and lay back on the pillow. "It'll be about six weeks to eight weeks before I can even think about climbing the scaffolding, and most of the work left in the barn is on the upper levels. I don't have insurance or savings. Everything I had left I put into the business with Reno, and now I can't work." Her breathing became labored again. "I'm completely dependent on my family. *Again.* Proving that I can't take care of anyone, including myself." She closed her eyes and threw her one free arm over her face.

No insurance? He could fix that. "If we got married, you'd be on mine."

Lowering her arm, her eyes went wide, and her mouth hung open.

He started sweating. "Not a real marriage, but one that's like a business deal. I can provide you with medical insurance and a place to live, and you would be in the house for the girls when they get home from school."

For a moment she just stared at him, then a deep frown marked her face. "Did you just ask me to marry you?"

The air in his lungs became solid, and he couldn't breathe. "Yes?" He managed to get out the one word. Why had that been his first solution to this problem? He was losing it.

Definitely not his greatest moment, but the need to help her was stronger than his common sense at this moment. His heart was thundering in his ears. He had vowed never to marry again. What was Savannah doing to him? Why had that been the first thing to pop into his head and right out of his mouth?

"Greyson, that's not a real solution. It's also fraud. What happens once I'm healed?"

They would be married. The idea of being husband and wife should have upset him, but it didn't. He could see them together. Getting ready for the day, having dinner and hanging out on the porch in the evening.

He shook his head. What was wrong with him? He should never want to share his life with someone else like that. He couldn't. He'd have to contact the Marshals.

She hated liars, and his whole life was a lie. He stepped back. The chair slid away from her when he fell into it.

"Greyson, are you okay? What's wrong? Well, other than you just made the most incongruous proposal ever." She grinned. "Please tell me you didn't ask your wife like this."

He hung his head. In a way, he had. They had been working on a business plan for a class they had together their senior year. He had turned to her and said, "We work well together. We should get married and make this a real business." Jessica had hit him over the head with her notebook.

She'd made him redo the proposal—the marriage one. She'd liked the business proposal. He brought his gaze up to meet hers. "I've always been practical. But you're right. I didn't think long-term. Sorry. Forget I said anything. You said you needed insurance and a way to live on your own. I'm sure we can come up with a better plan. I just want to help."

What he couldn't admit in a million years was that his heart liked the idea of being forever married to her. Sweat rolled down his spine. This was not good.

He made to get up, but her hand reached out to him. One gentle touch, and he was calmed. "I know your heart is in the right place, and I really appreciate it, but something like that would only work in fiction, not real life. I can't lie to the people I love, even for a good reason."

His heartbeat slammed into his chest. He shook his head, trying to clear his thoughts and emotions. It was all wrong. But at his core he knew it was what he wanted. To be married to her.

But he could never have it.

"My wife hit me over the head with our business plan the first time I asked her."

Her smile softened. "So confusing marriage and business is a long-standing issue?"

He grinned. "Yeah. I guess." Savannah was such a good person for his kids and for him. She deserved someone who could love her completely, without lying to her every day.

"The girls love you." That was safe, right?

She teared up. "I know, and I love them too. But look what happened. One day at the beach. It should have been fun and full of great memories. My family's right. I should never be responsible for children."

The fact that she still believed that had hot anger surging through his veins. "I thought you believed in absolute truth." He stood again and leaned over her bed. "You threw yourself into danger to save my girls. I would trust you with them over everyone else in this world."

The door opened, and she looked away from him. He took a step back. Her mother, two sisters, Margarita and Resa, along with her youngest brother came into the room.

"Oh, *mija*, you're awake." Her mother went to Savannah's bedside and set a fresh coffee on the table already full of hospital equipment, flowers and old cups. She touched her face with her work-worn hands.

"Greyson here has been waiting for you to wake up." She turned to him and smiled. "He's been very steadfast and devoted. Did you see the beautiful arrangement he brought you? I think it might be the biggest." Her eyes twinkled as she moved back to give her daughter her full attention. "You are a very brave girl, and I'm very happy that you have such a man in your life."

"Mother. Stop." From her bed, she turned to Greyson with a heavy scowl. "See? This is why your plan would never have worked. They already think we're an item. It would make it so much worse."

"What plan?" her mother asked.

"Yeah." Resa moved to the bottom of the bed and tugged at the foot of her good leg. She pulled up and adjusted the awkward yellow hospital sock that had slipped down the other. "Tell us about this plan."

"And why won't it work? We can help." Margarita, the oldest sister, stood next to their mother. Interest filled the eyes that matched everyone else's in the room. Their mother had stamped all her children.

Savannah sighed and flopped back on the bed, closing those deep, rich eyes. Waiting long enough to see that she wasn't going to talk, they all turned to Greyson. Reno leaned against the wall with a smirk and mouthed, "Sorry."

All the options ran through his head. He could tell them that he had just proposed. They would be all over that, and he knew without asking that he would have their support and help. Savannah would have no choice but to marry him. But that was not the way he wanted it to go down.

He took a deep breath and thought about what would be best for her. "I want Savannah to be my nanny and help out with the kids, but she says she can't be responsible for them because she lost Reno when he was little."

Her mother gasped, and the two sisters

rushed closer to Savannah's bedside. Standing with their mother, all three women wore the same frown. Reno straightened and came to the foot of the bed. Concern had wiped away his usual carefree expression.

With an uncharacteristic scowl, he glared at Savannah. "You still blame yourself for me running off? I've told you—" He scanned the room. His glare landed on each of the women in his family. "All of you, stop worrying about me and something that happened so long ago. I don't remember any of it." His hard gaze came back to Savannah. "Let it go. I couldn't be better!"

Savannah shook her head. "It's not just about you. I hurt the whole family. You don't remember, but everyone was so shattered that day. They brought in a dog and a helicopter. I overheard someone say they were looking for a body at that point. We thought you were..." Savannah closed her eyes. "Everyone knew it was my fault."

"Oh no, *mija*." Her mother pushed Savannah's hair back from her face. "We were very scared, but we didn't blame you. You were just a child. I should've kept him with me."

Her oldest sister had one arm around their distraught mother. "I let you both out of my sight. You were the last one to see him, so we kept asking you in hopes you would remember something new. You were never the one really responsible for him, I was. I lost him." Her oldest sister took Savannah's free hand into hers. "We never blamed you."

"I was in charge of him. Everyone was yelling at me, asking me questions I couldn't answer." Savannah looked at her mom. "You were crying so hard. It was the most terrifying moment of my life. Since then, y'all kept on saying I couldn't be trusted with children, and I was never asked to babysit."

"No. We never said you couldn't be trusted. And not asking you to babysit had nothing to do with Reno."

"Not on a conscious level, anyway." Resa frowned. "Maybe it had something to do with it in the back of our minds. But we didn't think you were unsuitable to be left alone with children. We didn't want to burden you."

"*Sí*," her mother agreed. "You were always different from my other girls who were born little mothers, caring for anything they could. You lived in your own world, not always connected to this one. I had just told you that you were in charge of him to give you something to do." Her mother twirled her finger in the air.

"You spent more time in the made-up world

in your head than in the real one with us. I blamed myself. We should have kept a better eye on him. I never wanted that burden to be yours." She cupped Savannah's face. "That's why we don't expect you to do all the domestic stuff. I was trying to protect you and let you be you without imposing expectations of being a housewife and mother." Her mother had tears streaming down her face. "I never meant for you to feel bad about it."

Margarita hugged her mom, then turned to Savannah. "That was a horrible day. We all felt we should have been watching out for you both. You've always been different, but not in a bad way."

Her oldest sister patted her arm. "Us protecting you from our kids' chaos wasn't because you lost little Reno. At one time or another, we've all lost him."

Her mother nodded and cut a motherly glare to the youngest at the end of the bed. "He never stayed where he was supposed to be."

Resa shook her head. "He needs a whole army looking after him."

"You know, I'm right here. And I happen to be a card-carrying adult that can drive and everything." He shrugged and grinned as only the youngest of seven would do. "Since we're talking about the thing we're never allowed to talk about, I want you all to hear this. Stop hovering. I'm a grown man."

Hands braced on the foot of the bed, he leaned toward Savannah. "You would make a great wife and mother." He grew serious and patted her good leg. "If I'm the reason you're holding back, stop it. And don't worry about the jobs. I know you are. I've called a few people, and I'm hiring them to help me finish. It'll cut a little into our profits, but not enough to do real damage. I've got you covered."

Her mother was staring at Reno, then jerked her gaze to Savannah. "This is the reason you think you can't be a good wife and mother? I just thought you didn't want to." Hugging Savannah, she gripped her close. "Oh, *mija*. I love you so much. I never meant to make you doubt yourself. I was just protecting you. You would make a marvelous mother. Greyson's girls love you."

Savannah stared at him over the smaller woman's shoulder. *Help me* was very easy to read in her expression. This was probably more than she could handle right now.

He looked at his watch. "I think they're about to come in to help her clean up. Why don't we go to the nurses' station and see if we can get an update?"

"Good idea." Her mother let go and stepped back. "I made the downstairs room ready for you. You won't have to worry about the stairs to the apartment. You'll be right next to me." She headed for the door with a new mission. "I'll need to get the care instructions to make sure you heal as fast as possible."

They filed out of the room. Greyson was the last one, but before he went out the door, she called him back. Surprised, he gently closed the door and went back to her bedside.

"I got the impression you were ready for us all to leave."

"Thank you for that."

He grinned. It felt good to help her this little bit. "No need. I could tell the emotions were getting too much. You like your quiet time, and your family is not always the best at picking up on that."

"Yes. But I also mean pushing through about Reno. I've always been too afraid to mention it. It seemed like it was an unspoken rule that we didn't talk about that horrible day. I really thought they all blamed me. I remember it so differently."

"That happens with childhood memories. Does this mean you'll think about my offer? The nanny one, not the wife gig."

She leaned forward. "My mother has the

room next to hers, ready for me." There was a panic in her eyes. "Once she gets me in there, I might never get free. Right now, I'm living with Reno in the apartment above the garage." She looked down at her leg. "I won't be able to climb the stairs."

"My other nannies had a room upstairs, but if you came and worked for me you could move into the apartment in the workshop. No stairs. Right now, all I need is for you to be home when my girls came in from school. I'd take them in in the morning and they could ride the bus home. If you were there to meet them, I could get so much more work done. You'd have insurance as my full-time employee, and you would be earning a wage. The living quarters, a nice one-bedroom apartment attached to a workshop that is ready for your creativity. We could both benefit from this nanny thing. The girls would love it."

His heart slammed against his ribs as though he had offered her marriage for real. He crossed his arms and studied the wedding ring he still wore. Why was her saying *yes* so important to him? Her saying *no* would be better for them both.

He raised his head to look at her and found she was staring at the same ring. Twisting the band, he knew it was time to put it away. He wasn't married to Jessica anymore.

With a half attempt at a smile, he looked at Savannah. "What do you need from me to make this a deal you can't refuse?"

"Can you tell me about your life before Port Del Mar?" Her eyes searched his face, pleading with him to trust her. To tell her the truth. His gut twisted, and his jaws locked shut.

And this was the reality of his life. He couldn't be the partner she needed. He would lose her before he ever had a chance to have her.

After a long moment of silence, she tried again. "Why did you move here to start a new farm?"

He wanted to growl as she pushed. Her chin lifted. She wasn't giving up.

She crossed her arms. "There's so much you're not telling me. Would you tell me everything if I promise to become your nanny?"

The fist that tangled his insides turned again. She wanted—deserved—the one thing he couldn't give her: the truth.

It was pure selfishness that he wanted to keep her in his life. He at least had to be honest enough to admit that it wasn't just for the twins. She had led him back to a life that could be filled with joy and true happiness. And love.

He should have walked out and let her go, but deep at his core, his instinct was to fight for her. This had to have happened to other people in the program. Maybe Diego had a suggestion. He had helped him find the farm.

"Savannah, this is a good temporary solution for both of us. The past has nothing to do with you taking care of my girls." He shrugged, trying to act as if it was no big deal, but he knew it was to her. She hated lies. "It's in the past, and that's where it stays. Tell me what else I can give you to stay with us."

"The truth. I need you to be open with me." She lay back on her pillow. There was an unbearably long silence between them. He wanted to tell her everything. That was not allowed. He tightened his jaw and crossed his arms again.

She sighed and closed her eyes. "I have to say no. I need what you can't offer."

He'd been afraid of that. With a nod, he left and closed the door behind him.

Chapter Eleven

Savannah stopped at the farm's front gate. A new sign hung over the entry. In beautiful vintage lettering, *Seeds of Faith* scrolled across the rich wood. The fields were a variety of greens ready to burst into color. Soon, Greyson would have his first crop, and then his work would really start. Preparing to harvest, sort and package the seeds had been his focus for the last few months, and it was going to pay off.

She'd barely made it a week at her mother's home. Her new downstairs bedroom that shared a wall with her mother, the lightest sleeper ever, had been a nightmare. Her mother was at her door asking what she needed if Savannah turned over in bed more than twice in thirty minutes.

Space. She needed space. She adored her

mother, loved her siblings, in-laws, *tías*, *tíos*, nieces, nephews and *primos*, but after a few days with this new level of care, she was looking for a way to escape. And she couldn't climb the stairs to her old apartment with Reno.

It had made her rethink all the reasons she had turned down Greyson's offer. He had a past he didn't want to talk about, but so did she. It was too emotional for him. He wasn't ready to talk about it. He might never be— and it wasn't her place to force him to.

Why did she fall in love with men who weren't available to her? Love. The realization yanked her up.

Argh. She dropped her head to the steering wheel. *Thunk. Thunk. Thunk.* Forehead pressed against the worn leather, she closed her eyes to stop the chaos swirling in her head and heart.

She loved a man who was obviously lying about his whole life. What was wrong with her?

Sitting up, she slipped the gear into Reverse. Greyson didn't trust her enough to share his life; he would never share his heart. Once again, she loved a man who would never love her back.

There was no way she could see Greyson

every day and not be filled with regret. Hiding at home with her mother might be a better choice. Five weeks next to her mother might push her to scream into her pillow every night, but it was better than crying.

A new song came on the radio. The words of the first line got her attention. It was all about doubt and regret. The singer went on to list all the negative words that she had been filling her own head with. She looked down the road to the house that called her. The song reminded her that even though life was hard and she had made mistakes, she was a child of the one true King. Was God asking her to trust Him on this path she kept coming back to? Was the truth in front of her or in her rearview mirror?

She'd go home and talk to her mother.

As she reversed out of the drive, she saw the back of the sign over the entrance. It was the mural the girls had painted on the porch the day she had arrived. Her throat tightened.

Now she was crying. Not for herself, but for those two young girls who needed her. They had called her to say how sorry they were, and they wanted her to come to the house. The place that felt like home to her.

It was one of the reasons she had packed her stuff while her mother was out and slipped into the car. Yes, she was a coward when it came to her mother. She could admit that. But was she a coward when it came to the journey God wanted her to take? Was she meant to be in the lives of those precious girls?

Phone in hand, she called her mom. *"Mami?"*

"Oh, *masita*. Where are you? The doctor said no driving. You should be resting. I've called all your brothers and sisters, and they're looking for you. *Todo esta bien?*"

"Everything is fine. I'm good. There were just too many people at the house wanting to help. I came out to Greyson's to take him up on his offer of watching the girls."

Her mother was silent for a moment, which scared Savannah. Her mother was never silent in situations like this.

"Mami, I don't know what I should do."

"You love him and those girls. God has put this in your heart. Where are you right now?"

"At his gate. He… There are things about his past that might not be right. I don't know if I can trust him or myself. But the girls need me. I know that. So I'm sitting here not sure if I should move forward or back. How do I know what God wants me to do?"

"That's a tough question. Give me a minute. There's a verse that I use in my meditation when I'm listening for God's will. Here it is. Romans 12:2. *And be not conformed to this world: but be ye transformed by the renewing of your mind, that ye may prove what is that good, and acceptable, and perfect, will of God.* You have been in the word of God. The church leaders have guided you in Sunday school. I know you say your daily prayers. Close your eyes and listen."

She prayed and opened her heart, not to her fears or what the world said, but what God placed there.

"I know what feels right. But what if it's me just wanting something I shouldn't?"

"Move forward with what you know for now. If it is not the road you should take, then God will reroute you. He can't open or close doors for you if you are standing still with your eyes closed. I was in that house with you. I, too, believe that is where you should be. If we are wrong, then God will close that door. I love you. And if you want to come back to the house, I will chase everyone away and give you alone time."

"Okay. Thank you. I love you too."

"You know if he had done anything illegal, your brother Bridges would have told you. He does background checks on everyone that you do business with. He would have warned you if there was something in his past to worry about. What are you going to do?"

"I'm going to talk to him."

"*Sí.* That is good. But you don't have to stay. We are here for you. You can come back to the room I made for you."

"*Gracias, Mami.* I'm going forward."

Disconnecting the call, she put her truck in Drive and followed her heart to Greyson's house. He had offered her a job, and she was going to say *yes* to that job.

Her heart was pounding in her throat. There was no reason to be nervous. He had been nothing but supportive and kind even when she let the girls get covered in mud or trapped below the jetty. No one had ever accepted her so unconditionally.

He had made it impossible to not love him. But that wasn't his fault. He had done nothing to mislead her. Greyson had been very upfront about his love for his wife and the fact that he had no desire to start a romantic relationship.

God had made it clear to her that she was the one putting up barriers to protect her heart. Greyson would never return those feelings, and she could live with that. She missed the girls more than she ever dreamed possible. He had said it was all for the twins, and she believed him.

It would be all about the girls for her too.

There was a strange SUV parked in front of the porch. Was she too late? Maybe he'd finally found a real nanny and didn't need her.

With a deep breath, she killed the engine. Before she could open her door, Greyson was on the porch. A woman was with him. Was she a nanny?

Probably. Greyson didn't have time to wait around. Her heart broke, and she wanted to cry. She *was* too late. He didn't need her.

He saw her and frowned. Well, that was not the reaction she had hoped for.

Great. Once again, she'd made the most awkward entrance. She could just back out and leave. Text him later and apologize for being weird. He said something to the woman, then started for her truck.

No way out. With a sigh, she opened her door. He was there before she could maneuver out of the truck. "Hi." That sounded weak.

"I thought you had orders to not drive?" He glanced down at her booted leg.

She hopped to the back of her truck and got her crutches from the bed. "I just need my right foot to drive. Your place isn't that far from Mom's." She took a breath, then bit

anything about your past. It's none of my business. I just want to take care of your girls while I heal. The real benefit is that I will not be sleeping next to my mother. And if the workshop is as good as you say it is, then I could get back to creating my art." She took a breath and looked at him. The silence was killing her. "So is the offer still good?"

A smile slowly spread across his face. "You see a woman on my porch, assume she's the new nanny, and now you want the job. Mistaking all women for nannies seems to be a problem around here."

She relaxed. "You do have a problem with keeping good help. I guess that's why you're the only person in the county who would even think of offering me a job watching kids. No beaches, though, unless you're there and in charge."

"Deal." He sighed.

He moved in like he was going to hug her. She stepped back and lost her balance.

"Sorry." He held her shoulders until she was steady, then took a big step back. "I'm, uh...really relieved you've agreed to help. I was trying to figure out how I could fulfill my commitment to Alvarado Farms and keep my girls safe. Thank you." He looked to the side and ran his hand through his hair. He was nervous. "I hope you find inspiration in the workshop. It's all yours."

"I want it to be clear that I'm only doing this through the summer, though. By the end of end of the school year I'll be back with Reno full-time, and I won't be working on the farm. That gives you plenty of time to find someone good. A real nanny."

"Savannah, I know you have no reason to trust me. But thank you for coming back. I'm picking up the girls in a couple of hours. They're going to the bakery after school. The girls are working on a group project about other countries. Will you go with me to pick them up?"

"I can do that."

"While we wait, do you want to see the workshop and apartment?"

"I do. But I think I need to get off my leg for a bit."

"Yes. I didn't think you should be driving." He rushed past her, then held his hand out at the steps. "Let me help you up. You can rest in the living room. The sofa is huge and has lots of pillows. You need to elevate your leg above your heart, don't you?"

She nodded as she took his offer of help. It would also be wise to kick him out of her heart. God placed her here for those sweet girls. Their father was carving his own place.

* * *

Greyson paused at the threshold. She was asleep. The desire to love Savannah and provide for her battled with what he knew to be true. He couldn't be that man. He had too many secrets he wasn't allowed to share.

The best he could do was speak in general terms, and even then, he had to be careful.

It was an impossible situation he had put them in, but his girls needed her, so he was going to have to tough it out. He hadn't even realized what they were missing until Savannah had stepped onto his porch. She had even opened his heart to the joy he thought was lost forever.

Adjusting the box he carried, he closed the door behind him.

She opened her eyes. "Sorry. I didn't mean to fall asleep."

"No. It's good. You're pushing yourself too hard. The body needs time and rest to properly heal." He put the box of supplies on the hallway table.

"Now you sound like my mother."

"She's a smart woman."

"Yeah. She is, and she knows it. So annoying. Thank you for letting me change my mind about your offer."

He sat on the club chair next to the sofa and

braced his elbows on his knees. Sitting like this, he was mere inches from her. "Do you believe that God puts us in places for a reason and that it's up to us to find that reason?"

She bit the corner of her mouth. The look in her eyes was so serious. "I've been thinking about that a lot lately. I don't have any clear answers."

He reached over and pushed back a strand of hair that had slipped from her ponytail. "My girls were missing so much because I had pulled back from life. I didn't see that until you came. You have given us so much. I want to give back and help you find your dreams. You showed me your sketchbook full of ideas. The apartment is attached to a workshop you can use as a studio whenever you're ready to create again. You can take those ideas off the page and become a professional artist."

Unexpected tears swam in her dark brown eyes. He cupped her neck and leaned in even closer. "That was meant to be a pep talk to inspire you, not upset you."

Savannah pulled back a little, and his hand dropped. She wiped her face with the blanket that had been on the sofa. "I've never had anyone truly believe that I could be a professional artist. My family loves my art, but they see it as a hobby. It's not something that pays bills or—" she lifted her hands and made air quotes "—lets me save for retirement."

He grinned. "I've always chosen unconventional ways to make a living, and I've been successful. I had naysayers. But J—my wife believed in me. Now I have a new venture. In another year or so I'll tell you how the wildflower-seed business turned out for me." He shrugged. "It's hard to take a chance on yourself. But I do believe we have an obligation to use the talents God has put in our DNA. Let my belief in you be your stepping-stone."

He rested his hand on her knee, just needing to touch her and reassure her it was going to work out. But he couldn't make that promise. Each morning he awoke knowing that at any moment disaster could steamroll his life.

What if he did tell her? He'd have to report it, and they would all be moved, but they could be together if she was willing to take a leap. Would she be willing to go with them, or would he risk it and still have to leave alone with the girls. His heart slammed against his chest. *Tell her.*

She shifted her weight, causing them to come closer together. She lifted her lashes, and they stared at each for a moment. The scent of wood and jasmine surrounded her and pulled him in.

She moved deeper into the pillows, away from him. "Every time I think I'm close to finding success or love, it unravels. It was so embarrassing to think I was in love, and he was just pretending. Thank you for offering to help me, but I can't stay here long. I'm messed up and weird." Her shoulders dropped, and she looked so alone and vulnerable.

He couldn't take it. She deserved all the love in the world.

"I happen to like weird." He grinned and lifted her chin until they had eye contact again.

He slid onto the sofa next to her and put his arm around her. "The people that did that to you took advantage of your big heart. You're so talented and an incredibly caring woman with more gifts than one person has a right to possess." Using both hands, he cupped her neck, his thumbs caressing her jaw. "You are a gift to anyone who has the privilege of loving you and sharing your life."

"But it seems that the ones I choose to love are never able to love me back."

An arrow went straight to his heart. Her lips parted slightly, and her eyes darted back and forth between his.

He couldn't hold back anymore. Not allowing any rational thought to alter his course, he slowly eased forward until their lips touched.

Savannah was everything he'd imagined: sweet, tender and soft. She was the home he'd lost. She was the place he wanted to land. She gently pressed into his touch, and for a moment everything was right.

But it couldn't be. He pulled away, looking anywhere but at her. He had kissed her. A few months ago, he would never have imagined kissing anyone other than Jessica.

Savannah had opened his heart to love again. But the world he lived in wouldn't allow it. She needed the truth, and he couldn't give her that.

Tell her. No. Her family was everything to her. She'd never leave them.

Standing, he cleared his throat. He should apologize, but the kiss hadn't felt wrong. He couldn't tell her it was a mistake because it had been too perfect.

He couldn't tell her the truth, but he was so tired of lying to her. The urge to punch a wall had his fist clenched.

Keeping his back to her, he stood in front of the large window that looked over the east side of the farm. He ran his hands through his hair, then crammed them into the front pockets of his jeans.

Something needed to be said, but he couldn't bring himself to spew another lie at her. "Sorry if I'm acting off. It's not you." He looked to the sky for any answers. "That was my first kiss since I lost my wife." His tongue ran over his bottom lip without thought. It burned in a way he'd never imagined experiencing again. The only touch he had known or wanted to know since he was eighteen was Jessica's. Until now. Savannah felt strange but so right.

Being in love with her wasn't good for either one of them. Gripping the window frame, he pressed his forehead against the glass. The darkness and helplessness threatened to drown him. Ripping his heart out so he'd never have to feel this loss again would be a fulfilled prayer.

"I'm so sorry." Her voice was low but broke through his black spiral.

He spun around to face her. Head down, she played with the corner of the blanket, folding it and unfolding it. She was feeling awkward. Shame was tattooed all over her body language. This was his fault.

"Don't." He moved toward her but stopped before he was in touching range. "There's nothing for you to apologize for. It just took me by surprise, that's all."

She looked so lost. He went to her and sat on the chair, making sure there was space between them. "If I could offer more to anyone, it would be you. There are things in my life that I have no control over." How could he even begin to explain without telling her too much? "It has nothing to do with you."

Chin up, she made a face and rolled her eyes. A begrudging smile pulled at the corner of his mouth. Her pride and stubbornness were stamped all over her beautiful face. Knowing that he had hurt her tore a piece of his heart out.

She drew back into the sofa, hurt radiating from her body.

He had said too much. He was making it worse. "Savannah?" He reached for her, wanting to make this right, but she jerked away, making it clear she didn't welcome his touch.

"We are adults and can admit to a mistake. Let's promise it won't happen again, and we can move on." With an awkward heave, she got off the sofa and wobbled a bit before getting her balance. Twisting, she tried to pick up her crutches. "I'm glad we had this talk. I understand things better now."

He frowned. "What things?" He picked up her crutches and handed them to her.

"Please. Just stop talking now." She closed her eyes for a second. "I want to leave. We need to pick up the girls. But I'm sorry. Me staying here won't work. I'll pick them up from school every day and stay until you get home. As soon as you walk through the door, I'll go back to my mom's. No family dinners together. No movies with the four of us." She turned and went straight for the door.

No. He wanted to yell the word out loud. He was losing her. What would it take to make her stay? The hopeful, stupid part of him said to run after her and yell that they were not a mistake. That kiss had brought him to life. She'd woken up his heart, and he knew he would never forget that kiss. He loved her.

But there was no way a relationship would work between them. Now he had to convince his heart of the undeniable truth his brain already knew.

He was half a man who couldn't even tell her his real name. The deep-rooted fear of failure dug into his chest, taking control.

He couldn't love again. The risk was too great.

Chapter Twelve

Parking in front of Pan Dulce, Greyson got out first and went around to help Savannah. They had been silent the whole way into town.

He opened her door, and Savannah put her hand into his without a fuss, but then she quickly pulled away.

The ground was uneven, and one of her crutches hit a crack. Gasping, she teetered sideways. Because he was standing close, he was able to catch her.

They were nose to nose. For a second, they just stared into each other's eyes. She shook her head and made a sound that could have been a forced laugh. He wasn't sure. Being close to her distracted him.

She patted his chest. "Now apparently *I* need a nanny. Do you know any good ones?" She leaned into him to get back on the sidewalk.

Unable to stop his smile, he kept his hand on her back as they moved to the bakery. "There's one in overalls who works wonders."

He opened the door for her, and a cheery little bell announced their arrival. As soon as the girls saw her, there was a great deal of jumping, screaming and hugging. Savannah had never felt so loved. Josefina brought out *cochitos* for everyone.

The molasses cookies shaped like little pigs were a hit with the girls. They had to make a deal that everyone was sorry about what happened and that everyone was forgiven so that the girls would stop apologizing. The plate was almost empty before they were calm enough to have a normal conversation.

On her knees, Abilene leaned over the table. "So you're our nanny? That's awesome. You can teach us how to fix things."

"Hey," Greyson said with a mock scowl. "I can show you how to fix stuff."

"Not as good as Savannah. She can fix anything," Evelyn said, in a very matter-of-fact voice. She grabbed another cookie.

"It's not long-term, girls. I'll pick you up from school while my bones heal. Then I'm going back to work with my brother."

"Oh. But our other nannies lived with us.

You can live with us forever, even if you're not our nanny."

"I don't want another nanny. I want you to take care of us when Daddy has to work."

"Girls, you should be grateful for the time you have with Savannah."

"We are, Daddy," Evelyn said, and her sister nodded. "And we pray every night that her leg'll get better and that she'll move in with us. Do you not want to stay because we didn't listen?"

"Oh no. I'm just going to help your dad while I get back on my feet. I love you both. But I can't move into your house. I have my own." Technically she didn't, but it was so much easier than explaining. She needed to set clear boundaries or she would have nothing left of her heart.

Abilene frowned. "You're out of the hospital, so you must be better. We'll keep praying so you can get the cast off."

"I know you're excited, but Savannah will do what is best for her. So please let her get some rest. She can't do that with all this noise."

"We're sorry."

"It's okay," Savannah told them. "Your excitement is making me very happy. But I also have other responsibilities. Your dad is going to find the perfect person to help watch you. I did talk to my sister also. She can help over the summer. You would get to hang out with your new friends. Desirae was very excited." How was she going to survive the next few weeks? She loved Greyson, but that could be dealt with.

The girls were her weakness. When she walked away from them, they would forever have a part of her. But she couldn't let them know. It was the worst, loving someone and not being able to tell them the depth of that love.

Once at the house, the girls jumped out of the SUV and ran to the steps. They stood at the door holding it open, waiting for her.

They were going to make her cry. She had avoided any eye contact with Greyson, but the twins did her in.

"Um, I have to go." She pointed to her truck.

"But you just got here. Please. Please. Stay just a little bit more," Evelyn begged.

"We've missed you so much and prayed for you to get better and come home." Abilene held her sister's hand. "Bliss and Finn have missed you too. You have to say hi to them."

"Girls." The deep, stern voice caused all three of them to jump. "When someone says they need to leave, you let them leave."

"Yes, sir."

"Sorry, Savannah."

The little shoulders slumped in total dejection. He was letting her leave. Did he not care enough to even try to get her to stay?

She couldn't leave the girls like this, not tonight. "You're right. I haven't seen Finn and Bliss. I've missed them. Have they gotten bigger?"

She put her crutch on the second step and tried to jump up but didn't make it. Greyson was at her side balancing her.

"You don't have to do this," he whispered.

"I know. But it's just for tonight. We hadn't really prepared them. Once we are clear about the expectations, they'll do better. See? I'm being a good nanny."

The smile he gave her was sad. As soon as she was on the porch, he moved away from her. It seemed he couldn't do it fast enough. What was she expecting? That he'd fall on his knee and ask her to marry him for real?

She was totally lying to herself if she thought she could do this without getting hurt. But if she was honest, then the damage would be minimal.

In the house the dogs came running. They seemed as excited to see her as the girls had been. There was lots of giggling and tail-wagging. The hole in her heart grew bigger.

But she knew the girls would be okay. Her mother and sisters would step in and do whatever was needed.

Greyson pulled a barstool with one of the sofa pillows next to another stool that he waved her to. "You need to sit and put your foot up."

"Does it still hurt?" Abilene was holding Finn. "Is there anything we can do to help?"

Bliss stood on her back legs, her paws gently touching Savannah's good leg. She patted her lap, and the pup jumped up. With big puppy eyes she looked up at Savannah. It seemed as if she was asking her to stay too. The person that mattered the most was not saying a word to her.

Greyson put a premade casserole in the oven. The girls set out ingredients to make a salad.

"Savannah, will you help us? We have carrots to cut." The twins pulled her into their conversation about school and who got in trouble for what.

Greyson did a great job of not directly looking at her or talking to her. That was good. It reminded her that he was off-limits.

The faster she came to terms with that, the better.

The evening went by fast and without any drama bubbling up between her and Greyson.

After dinner, the twins begged her to watch one movie with them. Their dad didn't seem to care one way or another. Okay… So he was over her. Great. That was how it should be.

"Okay. Tonight. But remember when I pick you up from school after this, I'm leaving as soon as your dad gets home. No dinner or movies."

"Why?" Evelyn's bottom lip stuck out. "We make a good family."

The air was trapped in her throat, and her eyes burned. Walking away from them was going to destroy her. Her gaze darted to Greyson. His jaw looked rock hard, and his lips thinned.

"Evelyn, you can't say things like that to people. Savannah is just helping us out. She has a family."

The little girl dropped her head. "I'm sorry."

"I'm here tonight. So let's make it a fun one, okay? What movie are we watching, and more importantly, who is making popcorn?"

"Daddy! Can you?" Abilene smiled at him.

"I'll be right back. Make sure Savannah is comfortable and has her foot propped up."

They took their job very seriously. She had pillows under her leg, behind her back and one to rest her arm on. They wedged themselves next to her. Bliss and Finn snuggled in tight.

Their dad came in and gave them each a bowl of popcorn. He sat close to Evelyn, one arm draped over her shoulders. If Savannah reached over, they could easily hold hands.

She closed her eyes. Why would she even think that?

If she had ever dreamed of a family of her own, it would look like this. How could Greyson give her a glimpse of a reality she hadn't even known she wanted? One that could never be hers?

Why couldn't it be hers? Because Greyson would never love her. He didn't trust her enough to share basic facts about his life. She didn't even know the name of his wife, the woman he still loved. It was foolish to think there could ever be anything. Her mother had said to follow what God wanted. Greyson made it clear she didn't have a place here, outside of helping with the twins.

The credits rolled. Stroking a short curl off Abilene's face, Savannah smiled at the sweet girl sleeping so soundly on her lap. She wanted to be able to fully love them, but they weren't hers. And Greyson had made it clear they would never be a family. It was time to walk away from him.

Greyson stood. "Do you mind staying here while I take Evelyn up?"

"That's fine."

With the older twin over his shoulder, he smiled at her. "I used to be able to carry them both up at once. Soon I won't be able to carry even one at a time to bed."

"My mom always says babies grow up when you aren't looking."

"It wasn't that long ago I carried them in from the hospital as newborns." He kissed Evelyn's head. "I'll be right back." Jumping off the sofa, the dogs followed him up the stairs.

Abilene shifted, getting closer to Savannah. Greyson and the girls had busted open a lie she had believed for too long. She had thought she was so different from her mother and sisters, but at her core she wasn't. *I would love to have babies of my own.*

In her mind, they were toddling behind the twins, trying to keep up with their big sisters. She shook the image out of her head. There were too many complications for that to ever happen.

Deep in thought, she jumped when Greyson touched her shoulder.

"It's just me," he whispered. He came around and dropped to his haunches in front of them. He smoothed back the same short curl she had been playing with. His tan hand looked so large against his daughter's little face.

He lifted his gaze from Abilene to Savannah. "They love you. Are you sure you can't spend the summer with us?"

She grinned or tried to, anyway. Her heart was a blob at the pit of her stomach. He didn't mean that the way it sounded.

If he asked her to marry him again, she probably would, but it would all be a lie. Shaking her head, she studied the soft features of the precious child that would never be hers. "I can't. I need to get on with my life. I'm sorry." Why was she apologizing about the truth?

Her fingertips were a butterfly's wing away from his very capable hands. "Your girls have a piece of my heart…but I can't stay."

She tilted her head and looked at the man she knew she loved with every part of her heart. Even the pieces she had hidden away. "I don't think there is anything else to talk about."

They held eye contact for a thousand breaths. He opened his mouth to say something, then firmly closed it. "Yeah." He scooped up the little body and stood. "Let me get the girls settled. I'll walk you to your truck."

Quietly, he disappeared up the stairs. Restless, Savannah grabbed her crutches and went to the porch. Her plan was to sit, but the darkness past the bright security light called her. Standing on the edge of the porch, she studied the night landscape beyond the safety of the well-lit yard.

Life was like this. The present was clear, but the future was full of the unknown. She had been staying safe within the walls she had built, not taking any risks with her creativity or her heart.

There were no guarantees. Fear of losing someone, fear of failure, fear of being hurt had all stopped her from really living.

When she had first entered Greyson's house, the unopened boxes had made her sad for him. But her whole life was a box begging to be opened, and she was ignoring it. He wasn't the one that needed to be fixed. She was.

She wasn't sure why she felt like crying. She loved Greyson and his daughters in a way she'd never experienced before. Trusting him would be the best thing she could do for herself. If he let her.

The door opened behind her. Greyson came

and stood shoulder to shoulder with her. "With no moon, it's dark out there tonight." He turned to her and took her right hand. "Savannah, you've brought so much light into our lives. I hate that I can't talk about my past and…"

Blood rushing through her veins, she waited for his next words. For more.

"Thank you." He stepped down and moved his hand to her elbow. "I understand why you need to leave. I'm sorry I can't… I can't offer you more. I… You make me want to offer more, but I can't."

And there he goes. Saying the words that melt her heart and turn her world upside down. This close, she could see the pain in his eyes.

He helped her balance as she went down the steps. His touch gentle, she needed to distract herself. "You don't realize how many steps are in the world until they become hard to manage."

"If you add that you just take them one at a time, it becomes an inspirational quote. A lesson we can all use to get through life." He held the truck door open and took her crutches once she slid behind the steering wheel.

"I know I've already said it, but thank you for helping with the girls. I know it's not your thing, but you're exceptional with them."

"They're easy to love." Too easy. "I'm serious about leaving as soon as you get home. The less time we spend around each other, the better. Josefina will be able to help with the twins over the summer. I might investigate an art program since I won't be able to climb scaffolding."

His hand tightened around the doorframe, but other than that there was no reaction. What was she expecting? For him to beg her to stay?

She should know better by now. "Good night, Greyson." She reached for the door and closed it, forcing him to step away from her.

It looked as if he lifted his hand to stop her, but then he dropped it. She backed up, then turned the truck around. Her gaze kept going to the rearview mirror until he was out of sight.

That's when the tears started to fall.

Chapter Thirteen

Greyson stood in the now fully restored barn. A week slipped by, and Greyson had played by Savannah's rules. As much as he wanted her to stay for dinner each night, he set his jaw, kept himself busy and let her walk out. What else could he do?

He could tell her the truth. Ask her to stay with them and complete their family. His head hurt, and his heart ached. How many people get two great loves in one life?

Alone in the barn that was now majestic in its soaring beauty, he fell to his knees and prayed.

"God, I beg you to remove this love from me if it's not meant to be." Falling forward, his elbows hit the cobblestone flooring, and he dropped his forehead into his palms. Losing track of time, he poured out everything to

God. He didn't move until his legs cramped in protest.

Shifting back, he lay on the floor and stared at the heavy beams above him. Rays of light caressed the restored wood. Particles of dust danced in the air, caught in the sun's brilliance. Endless blue sky could be seen through the widows high above the ground.

Savannah was in everything around him. Life was so precarious. Each day was unpredictable. He knew that better than anyone. A cloud floated over the skylights, casting a shadow. The tiny specks disappeared. He knew they were still there, but without the sunlight he couldn't see them.

Savannah was his light. God had given him this wondrous gift, and he was sending her away. He closed his eyes and let the silence clear all the clutter out of his brain.

A plan formed. He was good at plans. The Alvarado family could take over the farm. The girls were older, they would have a better understanding of what it meant to move to a new place with a new name. It would be up to Savannah if she wanted to go with them.

But the one thing he could not do was walk away from her without telling her he loved her and wanted to spend the rest of their lives together. But that meant he had to tell her everything. He couldn't offer her just parts of him.

She loved her family and might not want to leave. It was a big ask, but if he didn't, then he was being a coward. What if she did say *yes*?

With or without Savannah, he and the girls would start a new adventure. Maybe he could start a new business in Canada. He prayed that he was right and that Savanah loved him as much as he loved her.

Standing, he looked at his phone. Last night his girls had had their first sleepover with Josefina's daughter, Desirae. He was scheduled to pick them up in a couple of hours. That gave him enough time to lay out his plan.

Heart racing, he called Diego. He would know what he could and couldn't do. Then he'd talk to the twins and prepare them.

Before dinner he would know if Savannah was willing to give up everything for him and the girls or if they would be starting over, just the three of them.

The girls sat on the porch swing with the puppies in their laps. "So if we leave, we can help pick our new family name?" Abilene's eyes were bigger than usual.

Was he making a mess of this? The doubt and excitement twisted his heart. *Breathe*. His lungs had stopped working again.

If his plan worked out, Savannah would be leaving with them as his wife. *If.*

He hadn't been able to sleep last night, wrestling with the decision and how much to tell the girls.

He wanted them prepared to leave but he didn't want to get their hopes up about Savannah going with them.

The dogs were as still as the girls. That made him nervous. "You'll finish out the school year, but then they'll move us to a camp where we will learn our new identities. I don't know if you remember the last one."

Evelyn pressed her lips together and frowned. She scanned the area over his shoulder before meeting his gaze. "We didn't tell anyone about Mommy or our other name. We didn't break the rules, Daddy. We didn't tell Savannah, even though she said it was safe to talk to her." Evelyn held Bliss close, and the dog licked her cheek. "We get to keep our first names. Can Finn and Bliss? They might not understand if we call them something different."

"They can keep their names. I'm the one that broke a rule." He hadn't yet. If he didn't tell Savannah his story then they wouldn't have to leave, but Savannah could never truly be a part of their lives.

It would be painful to stay here and ignore the feelings he had for her. It would be hard on the girls too.

For now, it was about keeping them safe and getting them to adulthood with as few emotional scars as possible. Everything inside him said Savannah was the key for the girls and himself. To be loved and to love someone. Loving unconditionally was a gift he could not set aside.

"What about Savannah. She loves us, and we love her. It will make her sad if we leave." For the first time, Evelyn looked as if she might cry.

Abilene put and arm around her and leaned on her shoulder. "Can we ask her to come with us? If you get married, she'd keep our secret."

His nervous system numbed his whole body for a moment. Not knowing how to answer that he just shook his head.

Today. He had to speak with her as soon as possible. There wouldn't be any sleep or a moment of peace until he knew how she felt.

He prayed his faith in Savannah's love for him and the girls was not misplaced.

Abilene sat up. "Ask her. She loves you a whole bunch. Tell her we'll be good listeners."

Evelyn nodded in agreement. "We promise to do whatever she tells us. The first time." They were so earnest, he wanted to wrap them up tight and hold them close so the world couldn't hurt them.

"This has nothing to do with you. You understand that, right?" Was he making it all worse? No, he had to trust God that this was the right thing, and he would go in with all the confidence he used to take for granted. "We will always have each other, and most importantly, God has you."

They nodded.

"Right now, I need you to clean up your playroom." After hugs they went inside the house. With a task in hand, hopefully they'll stay busy long enough for him to call Savannah and find out her location.

He hit her number, but Reno answered. "Hello?"

"Reno?" He frowned. "I thought I'd called Savannah."

Reno laughed for a long moment. "Sorry." He coughed. "You did, but Mom took her phone away to make her rest." He chuckled again.

Greyson wasn't sure what was so funny about this conversation.

"I don't think I'm supposed to know this." Reno lowered his voice. "But you're saved in her phone as *The Most Interesting Man Alive* with double hearts. That's why I had no clue who was calling." He cleared his throat, all humor gone. "Man, she must have it bad for you. I hope you get your act together. I really like you, but what's been going on? Am I going to have to call my big brother and pay you a visit?"

"I'm calling her because I need to see her. Where is she?"

"She's here at my mom's house. But warning. Every Espinoza in the county is here. If you're coming to declare yourself, you will have an audience. If you do something to hurt her, all goodwill is gone."

Sweat rolled down his spine. *I was hoping to take her away forever.* This had to be done right. The Espinoza family wouldn't allow her to just disappear. He hadn't thought of that. He had to find a way to get her alone. This was getting too complicated. But what else did he expect?

"Can you give her the phone so I can talk to her?"

"Nope. My mom would not be happy with me."

Greyson sighed. "Could you tell her to come to my house?"

"Nope. My mom again. Dude, you're going to have to come over here."

No, no, no, no, no. New plan. He'd pick her up and take her somewhere private. Maybe someone in her family would watch the girls. Okay. He could do this.

"Tell her I'm coming over." Slipping his phone in the back pocket of his jeans, he went to get the girls.

Reno had *not* been exaggerating. The street going to the Espinoza house was lined with trucks and SUVs. There might have been one or two regular cars, but overall, it was a collection of Texas-size vehicles. He drove past the house and found a spot in front of her sister's home a few lots down.

Deep breaths had not slowed his racing heart.

"Is it a party, Daddy?"

"Nope. Just an Espinoza family dinner." All the doubts came rushing back. Why would she leave this for him?

Please, God, give me the right words.

With a forced smile, he nodded to the girls and got out of his Traverse. The twins walked beside him. They took his hands as they held on to Bliss's and Finn's leashes. The dogs trotted in front of them.

On the porch, the door opened before he could even lift his hand to knock. Yolanda's face lit up. She wiped her hands on her apron, then hugged each of them. She even greeted the dogs. "*Vienes adentro.* Come in." She stepped back.

The house was full of people. Kids sat on the floor playing a game. There was a basketball game on the TV. Several of the family members wore Spurs jerseys. Ginobili seemed to be the most popular player among this crowd even though he was retired.

Yolanda introduced him to everyone. They greeted him, then went back to the game. "Come. You came to see your Savannah."

He hoped she was his, but that would depend on her. They went through a busy kitchen where he was hugged and welcomed and offered food. The girls were given something to eat. Past the kitchen they stepped down into a seating area with several tables set up with bowls and corn husks. Finally, he saw Savannah.

She was on a couch, her foot up and a frown on her face. The room was just as crowded as the others.

"We are making *tamales* for several birthdays coming up," Yolanda said to explain the chaos. "But you are here to see Savannah, *sí*?"

Savannah's eyes went wide when she saw him. "Greyson?" She pulled herself up. "What—"

"She has been working too hard so I made her lie down. No phone."

The girls and dogs rushed to her, showering her with hugs, kisses and a few excited barks. She laughed. "It's great to see you too."

A smile radiating on her face, she looked up at him, then grew serious. "What's wrong?" She was still petting the dogs and had the girls pulled in tight. They looked like a unit that belonged together.

"It's all good. I came to ask you something."

The room went dead silent, and all movement stilled. "Um, could I...take you somewhere to talk?"

Yolanda motioned for everyone to get back to work then turned to Greyson. "Her leg is all swollen. She can't leave, but..." Going to the back of the room, she opened a door. "The patio is very private."

Greyson helped Savannah to her feet. She wobbled and grimaced in pain. He wanted to take her somewhere, anywhere, but that was not a possibility with her mother hovering.

For a moment they stood an inch apart. He knew he was doing the right thing. She belonged in his life, and he belonged to her.

Yolanda chased the people off the patio. They smirked as he helped Savannah to a cushioned rocking chair.

With everyone cleared out of the area, Yolanda turned to him. "I'll keep the girls inside. I'll put them to work with the cousins." With a sly smile and nod, she quietly closed the door behind her.

He pulled one of the camp chairs next to her and took her hand. The knot in his throat made it hard to speak.

"Greyson? What's going on?"

"Your brother said you had me listed as *The Most Interesting Man Alive* with a couple of hearts on your phone contact."

She turned red and lowered her face. "That's embarrassing. He's going to pay for that."

"Savannah, I think you are the most interesting woman." He took a breath. "I love you."

Her mouth fell open, and she blinked. "I…"

He shook his head and gently pressed his fingers against her soft lips. "Don't say anything yet. I'm going to tell you everything about me, then you have a decision to make. It won't be easy. Just know I'm doing this because I love you."

She nodded and waited.

"My wife was shot in front of me on our anniversary. She was shot by a man that the government had been wanting. Her murder had nothing to do with his cartel. It was personal. She had testified that he was an unfit father. After the courts took away his children, he blamed her and murdered her in retaliation. Even though it was separate from his organized crimes, they saw it as a way to get him behind bars. I became their key witness. I had to relive Jessica's death in court."

She touched his cheek. "Your wife's name was Jessica."

"It's the first time I've said it outside of that courtroom. I became their biggest piece of evidence and had to go into the federal witness protection program to protect the girls. I'm not allowed to say anything about my past."

"But you're telling me."

"I love you, and I want to have a chance of us being together. Now that I've exposed who I am, the girls and I have to leave. They'll be relocating us once school is out."

She gasped. "Then, why did you tell me?" Tears spilled over. "You have to leave town."

"Because I wanted to ask you to leave with us."

She sat back, stunned.

"Let me tell you the whole story, from the day I met Jessica to now. Can I do that?"

Savannah was unable to speak, so she cupped his face and nodded.

He did. From his earliest memories to the day Jessica changed his life. Then the life they had built and the end of it. Everything that brought him here to this moment.

"Savannah, all I have to offer is broken pieces, but I know one thing without a doubt. I love you, and all these parts of me that are jagged, shattered and stitched back together by God are now yours, if you'll have me."

Tears trailed down her cheeks. "I love all those beautiful pieces. When I came home, I promised God I would trust Him with everything and not trust anyone else. I closed myself off and blamed it on God. But it was me. We're all flawed and broken in some way." Her thumb caressed his face. "I had it all wrong."

Words and thought swirled in her head. She sat back to give herself some space. "I thought I was making myself stronger by not letting others in. I had convinced myself that I didn't want a family. Cut myself off from all of God's real plans for me in order to protect myself. My life was like one of your unopened boxes. I had put my whole life in a box and sealed it up. You helped me find the faith to open them."

He reached across the space separating them and took her hand. "You were so full of life and willing to share it with us. It was your bravery that opened life for me again."

Smiling, she leaned forward and cupped his face. "It was God."

Moving quickly, he took her in his arms, pressed his lips to hers. After a moment, he took a breath and leaned his forehead against hers. "Savannah Espinoza, I love you. I want you to be in my life every single day. Will you run away with me and the girls?"

She pulled back.

"I love you too. I can't imagine my world without you in it. Or the girls. But I…my life is here. Everything. My business. My family."

It was too fast. "I don't know." Blood was rushing through her body, and she couldn't catch her breath.

His features tightened, and he sat back in the chair. "I'm sorry. I have no right to ask you to leave your family. I don't know what I was thinking."

He ran his fingers through his hair and stood.

His story. Her leaving with them. All the

information and choices created a whirlwind in her mind.

"Now that I've told you everything, we'll be relocated. Please, for the safety of the girls I beg you not to say a word of this."

"Of course." She stood, wanting to go to him, but not sure what to do. "What would happen if I did go with you?"

Spinning on his heels, he turned to her. Deep lines creased his forehead. A painful silence stretched between them.

He cleared his throat. "If you go with us, there will be no contact with your family. Only your mother and siblings can even know we're in the program *after* we leave. No good-byes, or family pictures. They can't know where we are or our new name. There's no coming back."

She closed the distance and gripped his hands. "I do love you, but… It's big. How would we start?"

He licked his lips and nodded. "We'd have a quick wedding here, then leave on our honeymoon. That would be it. They'll send us to a safe place, where they will get us a name and all new paperwork to go with it. We'll never come back. It'll be up to your family to make a plausible reason we don't return. I'll turn the farm over to the Alvarez family."

She closed her eyes to process all the ramifications.

Greyson went to his knee. His fingers gripped hers, not to tight, but enough to let her know he would always hold on to her if she allowed.

"It's not fair to ask you to walk away from everything you know, but I promise to love you. Your light filled my life in ways I never imagined. I'm not sure I have anything even close to offer you."

"You." She would not cry. "You ripped the tape off my boxes, and I finally know who I am. Not who my family thinks I am. Not the town. I found the real me. That was because of you."

"My heart tells me we belong together. But you need to be sure. If you decide to stay here. I understand. The girls and I will go knowing you loved us. That's enough."

She slid into the chair and leaned forward until their foreheads touched. "I'm not sure it's enough for me."

"What do you want?" His voice was rough.

"Without meaning to, I think my family keeps closing me in a box. I want out. You see me. My heart is telling me you are my best future. But I'm scared."

He nodded. "You don't have to commit

right now. The girls know we are leaving, but they don't know I'm asking you to go with us. They told me to." He chuckled. "But I didn't want to hand them another disappointment. And you didn't deserve that kind of emotional blackmail."

"They want me to go with you?"

"Of course. They love you as much as I do. But really—"

This time she placed a finger against his lips. "Everyone knows I'm the flighty one. My mother will do anything in her power if it'll make her children happy. I have no doubt she would make up a grand adventure for us. If she says it, the whole town will believe it." She looked down at their joined hands. "You and the girls are my family." When she looked back up at him, moisture glistened in her dark eyes. Eyes he could get lost in. "I'm in."

"Are you sure?"

"I love my family, but I think to really find myself I need to leave."

"It'll be forever. Do you trust me enough to do this?"

She nodded. "I'll trust you with my heart and my future."

He wrapped her in a warm hug. Pressing his lips to her ears, he whispered, "I love you.

Thank you for trusting me. We'll find a way to build you a studio and make your dreams come to life."

Turning her head, she kissed his jaw. "Mr. Greyson, you're my dream come true. Everything else we can deal with as it comes. I love you. My mother will be so mad that I didn't warn her beforehand. How will she find out?"

"Once we're gone, we'll write her a letter explaining that we are in the program, and we won't be returning. The US Marshals will read it to make sure it's safe, then deliver it to your mother. Once she reads it, they'll destroy the letter. She can respond if she wants, and once you read the letter, it too will be destroyed. No link between us can exist. Are you sure about this?" His hands on her arms, he leaned back and studied her face.

With a nod and a smile from her, he relaxed for the first time since she saw him walk through the door. "I promise to love you every day. You are my heart and everything good about me."

She cupped his face and brought him in for a kiss. "I gave you all of me and all of my love weeks ago."

Pulling her to her feet, he held her close. Jasmine and vanilla surrounded them. His lips touched the soft skin next to her ear. "Then, it seems we have a wedding to plan."

"And an adventure to start."

Epilogue

Greyson leaned against the doorframe and took the time to watch his wife work on her latest project. She was so focused she hadn't heard him walk in the studio. The edge of the driftwood she had found on the beach was balanced on her belly.

At seven months their baby boy was definitely making his presence known. Just a few weeks ago she had been complaining she didn't look pregnant. She might be regretting that now.

His phone chirped, but she didn't even notice. With a grin he checked the text. It was from his newest client. Instead of working outdoors, he now designed and built self-maintaining eco-friendly habitats inside homes and buildings. The latest contract was with a hospital.

"Daddy! Mom." Evelyn ran across the connecting passage from the house. Abilene and the dogs, now all bigger than when they moved in, were right with her. "There's a man at the front door. He looks very serious. We didn't answer it."

Savannah looked up. "Who's here?"

"Probably nothing. Wrong house or some survey. I'll check it out. Stay here with Savannah." The girls nodded as Savannah stood to be next to them. They all looked very worried. No one ever came to their house. "Girls, it's okay."

He went to the kitchen and saw the girls had been in the middle of making smoothies when they saw the guest. Crossing the room, he looked at the security screen that had told the twins someone was here. Air stopped flowing through his lungs.

It was Diego. This couldn't be good. Had something happened to Savannah's family? Was there a new threat?

His stomach turned at the thought of leaving this perfect little spot in Washington state. With a deep breath, he made his way to the front door. His hand rested on the doorknob for a moment before turning it. He knew life was uncertain, and they had made sure to live it to the fullest. Was it all about to change?

Now he was being a coward. With a yank he opened the door to whatever news the Marshal had brought.

"Hey, Greyson."

"Diego, come in." He stepped back. "What brings you to our door?" It had always been a call.

"Maybe some good news for your family." The man grinned. Greyson had never seen the federal officer smile.

"Should I get Savannah? The girls?"

"No. You can tell them. But you'll be able to make some new decisions."

Greyson blinked. "What's going on?"

"Carlos Lopez was killed in prison."

The man that had killed his wife was dead. Greyson wasn't sure how he should feel. Right now, he was numb. "What does this mean?"

"There has been a shift in the hierarchy of his little gang. The hit on your wife was a personal vendetta, so the threat to you and the girls died with him. You aren't on any of those guys' radar. You can stay here and continue with the life you have, or you can return to your old life. I see no reason that stops you from reaching out to your families. The girls can have pictures of their mom." He shrugged. "I mean, don't go yelling from the rooftops that you helped put away Carlos Lopez. You know, be smart."

Greyson nodded. "Are you sure? He's dead."

"Yes. I wanted to tell you in person. If you have any questions, you know how to reach me."

Greyson followed him out and watched as the black sedan pull out of the quiet neighborhood. When he went back into the house, his three girls were standing in the archway to the kitchen.

He smiled. "We're free."

They all tilted their heads in confusion.

"The man who killed your mother is dead. The threat is gone."

Abilene picked up Finn. "Does this mean we are moving again?"

He looked at Savannah. "It can mean whatever we want it to mean."

Savannah moved forward and took his hand. "So we can call my family. We can visit them."

"Do you want to stay here?"

She looked at the girls and back at him. "You're my home." There were tears in her eyes. "I would like to visit my mom. And my sisters and brothers. Maybe have the baby in Port Del Mar with Resa. I would really like that." She looked at the girls.

"We miss Texas."

Abilene nodded. "Can we go back to our farm?"

He pulled his family close. "If it's Texas you want then Texas it will be."

They tightened their grip around him, and for a moment it was a tangle of arms, tails, kisses and hugs. This was his family. No matter where they were or what name they went by, his heart was at home with Savannah.

"I love you," he whispered in her ear.

She turned her face toward him and kissed him, and he could feel all the love she had for him. She was his home.

* * * * *

Dear Reader,

Thank you for hanging out with Savannah and Greyson. This book is the first of a new series, Lone Star Heritage. A few years ago, I visited the WildSeed Farms in Fredericksburg, Texas, and fell in love with the idea of setting a story on a wildflower farm. I was also intrigued by living in the witness protection program *after* the court case was over. Have you ever tried to research something whose whole goal is to remain secret? The information can be a bit contradictory. LOL.

Savannah and Greyson both had ideas of who they were from other people and circumstances in life. When they finally leaned fully into God, they were able to find their true essence. It's a journey that I enjoyed taking them through. Trusting God completely is so much easier in certain parts of our lives. Trust and wisdom to understand is something I pray about every day.

I love connecting with readers. You can email me at jolenenavarroauthor@gmail.com or get updated information by subscribing to my website, jolenenavarrowriter.com.

Thank you,
Jolene Navarro

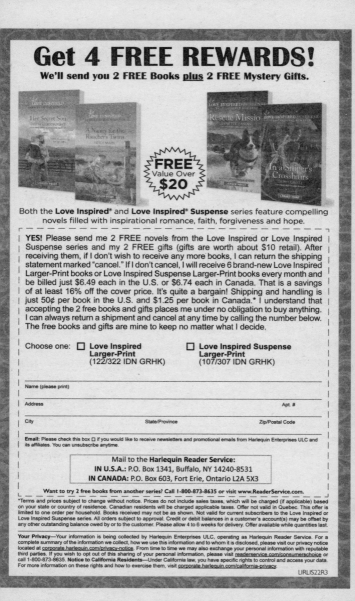

HARLEQUIN
PLUS

Try the best multimedia subscription service for romance readers like you!

Read, Watch and Play.

Experience the easiest way to get the romance content you crave.

Start your **FREE TRIAL** at
<u>www.harlequinplus.com/freetrial</u>.